PUBLISHER/EDITOR
K. Allen Wood

CONTRIBUTING EDITORS
John Boden
Catherine Grant
Barry Lee Dejasu
Zachary C. Parker

COPY EDITOR
Sarah Wood

LAYOUT/DESIGN
K. Allen Wood

COVER DESIGN
Mikio Murakami

Established in 2009
www.shocktotem.com

"Night in the Forest of Loneliness" first
appeared in *Bards and Sages Quarterly, Vol. 3,*

Issue 2, Bards and Sages Publishing, 2011

"The Candle Eaters" first appeared in *The Gate 2: 13 Tales of Isolation and Despair*, T.R.O. Publishing, 2012

ISSN 1944-110X

Printed in the United States of America.

Notes from the Editor's Desk

Welcome to the third *Shock Totem* holiday issue!

The big one. Halloween. Little more need be said. If you're a fan of horror, this is your holiday, and this is our tribute...

Treats abound, in this special edition of *Shock Totem* are seven short stories, one poem, and five nonfiction pieces. Of the fiction, **John Boden** and **Bracken MacLeod** venture into dark and weird neighborhoods in "Halloween On..." In "Out of Field Theory," **Kevin Lucia** gives us a shadowed glimpse of what lurks beyond the frame. **David G. Blake's** "Night in the Forest of Loneliness" smells of autumn and the beautiful death she brings.

Learn why sometimes it's better to stay home on Halloween in "Tricks and Treats," by **Rose Blackthorn**. **Kriscinda Lee Everitt's** "Howdy Doody Time" is a poignant nod to the past. The shadows come alive in "Before

This Night Is Done," by **Barry Lee Dejasu**, and in my story, "The Candle Eaters," I explore faith and hope and a darkness that haunts us all.

In addition to the fiction, **Sydney Leigh** provides a very fine poem, "Allhallowtide (To the Faithless Departed)."

Authors **John Langan**, **Lee Thomas**, and **Jeremy Wagner**, as well as filmmaker **Mike Lombardo** and the always wonderful and brusque **Babs Boden**, provide anecdotal Halloween recollections.

And there you have it, folks. The quick and dirty. No tricks, all treats.

Dig in!

K. Allen Wood
October 31, 2014

Contents

Halloween On...

by John Boden and Bracken MacLeod

The porches sag and creak, weary from all their burdens. The jack-o-lanterns glow and smile wide and wider, waxen tongues of flicker and flames dance behind them. Molten wax hisses when it licks the wick in sizzle kisses. Bats flutter and dance in the dim shine of streetlight as they devour insects by the pound. Giggles and squeals mingle with them.

The children wander and run. Stumble and fall. Sweaty fists around paper sacs or plastic bags. Mouths moist with candy and spit. Tripping on cloaks and capes and toilet-paper bandages. A miniature army of ghoulies, ghosties, and long-leggedy beasties. They scour the neighborhood until every house has been hit, more than once, their bags bulging with candy and gluttony. Eyes glisten with every emotion save for dignity.

Roger stares out the kitchen window and smiles. It is not an honest smile. He turns to the tableful of candies, small chocolate blobs, each resting upon their original wrapper. He quickly wraps each one and wipes them off the table edge and into the plastic cauldron. He sets it on the counter and puts the drain cleaner and Borax under the sink, the sewing kit back on the hall table. He looks into the mirror above it and straightens his collar. The tiny square of white lining perfectly with his square jaw. He fastens the top black button, then grabs the candy and heads for the porch.

His hand shakes a little as it hovers in front of the switch for the porch light. He closes his eyes, nods, and flicks the switch. Pale yellow light illuminates the porch and walkway. Children shout and footsteps assault his ears before he even fully gets out the door. "Trick or treat, father!" So loud. Tiny hands darting for the mouth of the container. Father Brigham looks up at the stars and smiles again. "Only one apiece, please," he says.

There's salvation in the air and it smells like cinnamon and leaves.

The Corner of Cave and Ellis

Nick tugged at the costume where it

bunched up. He'd spent hours on it, but it still didn't fit quite right, riding high in the crotch and twisting around uncomfortably in other places as he moved. He didn't move much, though. He stared at the computer and shoveled another handful of puffs into his mouth. His mom had asked why he went to all the trouble of making a costume if he wasn't going out. He said he'd go later, after the crowds died down. She treated him like a little kid, telling him he'd miss all the best candy. It never occurred to her that everyone would think it was weird that a fifteen-year-old dressed up. He never admitted he couldn't bear to hear the other kids laughing at him or the adults scolding him for being too old for Halloween.

On the screen, Mr. Bowman's head popped in a fountain of red. The rifle report passed through Nick's headphones, echoing in the night of ones and zeros. A chime sounded and a glowing double-digit score rose up out of the ragged stump of Bowman's neck. Juanita Bowman was so gorgeous he ached when he thought about her. Nick paused, making his avatar crouch over the collapsed body—tea-bagging it. Achievement unlocked! He moved on, continuing to virtually prowl the streets of South Yardley.

Homeshores wasn't the best shooter. It had decent graphics and the gameplay was all right, but it had open source code and the creators encouraged mods. He'd mapped the entire neighborhood, spending months capturing every house along the way with his dad's Minolta. That online satellite program helped him map the back yards. He took pictures of the people in the division too: Lester Little and his zombie wife, the Bowmans, that asshole priest, and the Stouts down the cul-de-sac. He already had all the kids' faces from the annual. He encoded everyone in the neighborhood except old Mrs. Hearn. She was sweet to him. He didn't need to shoot her.

BLAM! HEADSHOT!

Barry Grant went down.

Downstairs, his parents laughed at some idiot sitcom.

A bunch of eggs slapped and splattered against his window. He started, terrified and gasping. His spasming hands tangled up in the headphones cord and pulled them painfully off.

Nick breathed, trying to slow his heart. If he couldn't remain calm under pressure it was never going to work. He didn't bother looking out the window. It didn't matter who threw the eggs; they were all the same.

He brushed the tears off his face and wiped them on the FDNY patch stitched over his heart. Someday he'd be a protector. He'd be a hero and rescue people. But first he had to learn not to be afraid of them. He'd never be brave enough to run into a burning building if stepping out the door gave him a heart attack.

He sat down again and picked up his imaginary rifle, ready to confront his fears.

The Corner of Ballard Ave

Bonnie sat at the small table in the display window of what used to be the town General Store. She'd wanted to convert that space into a reading nook—something homey and comfortable—but Lester wouldn't allow it. He'd insisted on the table and chairs, arranging them to present the appearance of a place where customers could sit and moon over each other as they sipped at twin straws from the same malted milk glass. Except, she wasn't allowed to sit there. No one was. "It's about the ambiance," he'd say. "We've got to preserve the aesthetic of the original."

She stared out the window at a group of children over at Father Brigham's. A faint choral "Thank you" echoed through the neighborhood. The kids bounded up Ash Street, giddy in the night. A small contingent of adults trailed them from a respectful but safe distance. Bonnie thought how nice it was to live in a place where parents would let their kids come out after dark.

She watched them move from house to house until finally reaching hers. Trick-or-treaters never came to her door. Lester would turn the porch light off and say, "Store's closed." He only wanted the appearance of a public place; in reality, their house was a complete departure from anything one might call welcoming.

Not this year.

Bonnie jumped up at the sound of the bell. She cheerfully sing-songed, "Trick or treat!" as she flung the door wide, beating them to the punch. She complimented the kids on their costumes, making sure to let each one know how impressed she was by their originality.

"You did a great job decorating," Juanita Bowman said.

Bonnie had hung orange and green string lights around the windows and draped a purple bat-shaped garland from the eaves above the door. A black and orange wreath decorated the window in the door and she'd even squeezed herself down into the crawlspace beneath the front deck to set up the sound effects speaker playing a loop of ghostly wailing and cats yowling over a soundtrack of spooky organ music. The sounds carried up from between the boards along with the faint hint of her husband's screaming.

"Thank you."

"Lester's not around?"

Bonnie listened to him using up the last of his oxygen. It had been so hard to dig down there. The earth was dry hardpack. After a foot or so, she was able to dig from a kneeling position, but the extra room didn't translate into less work. It was a slow hell all the way down. But he was roofed and locked in the box; she'd had time to dig it just right. She imagined she might have gotten three or so feet down at the end of it. Deep enough.

She wanted to hear.

More than that, she wanted him to hear the children screaming "Trick or treat!" She wanted him to hear them laughing and her telling them all, "You're welcome."

The Corner of Kenwood Lane

Missus Hearn watches her game shows alone. She steals looks at the bowl of candy on the small table by the door, sees the tarnished patina of porch-light glowing through the screen door, and sighs for the thousandth time. She stands with a groan and walks over to peer out at the empty street. "I remember when my boys was little, there was easily eighty kids for trick or treats." The statement is meant for no one, so the fact it is mumbled through a mouthful of chocolate matters not. She balls up the foil wrapper, pushes it to the bottom of the bowl with the others, and returns to her chair.

Pat Sajak is looking weird these days; he's probably had some work done. She shakes her head and thinks about turning off the porch light and calling it a night. She thinks she sees a shadow on the porch. *Was that a small knock?* With the popping of knees and groaning of back, she rises, walks over to the door, and looks outside.

Nothing.

The chair beckons, promises warmth for her aching back, comfort for the evening. She turns—but there it is again, another feeble knock on the door. This time she's sure. She smiles and whispers, "Finally."

The boy is small, very small. Possibly three years old. He has dark brown hair, cut in a bowl that crowns his chubby cheeked face. "Hello there." She nudges the door open with an elbow. The boy smiles and hold up his pillowcase. *A pillowcase?* Boy, that takes her back. "Well, I haven't had many kids tonight and I'm tired, so I'm gonna give you a few handfuls, okay?" He nods excitedly, and she grabs a handful of candy and drops it into the boy's pillowcase.

Ronald, her oldest son, sits in his car across the street. His face is wet with tears. The cell phone to his ear rings again and then someone picks up. "Tim," he says, "I'm watching mom hand out candy. She just dropped about five handfuls into...well, nothing. There isn't anyone there. She just opened the door and stepped out onto the porch. She's smiling and talking to someone, dropping candy on the porch." He sighs and sniffs back tears. "I think we need to call that lady at the care place—it might be time."

There is a long pause that stings like bees.

"I'm on my way," Tim says.

Ronald drops the phone on the passenger seat. He covers his eyes with a pink hand and cries quietly in the dark.

On the porch, his mother waves to the little boy who made her night. Reminding him to be careful as he goes down the steps, and to stop at the car beside the street sign and give a piece of candy to her son, Ronny, to cheer him up. The moon sat in the sky like a blind eye.

John Boden lives in the shadow of Three Mile Island, where he bakes cakes and cookies for a living. Any remaining time is unevenly divided between his amazing wife and sons, working for Shock Totem, and his own writing. His unique fiction has appeared in *52 Stitches, Metazen, Weirdyear, Black Ink Horror 7, O Little Town of Deathlehem, Radical Dislocations, Splatterpunk 5*, and *Psychos*, edited by John Skipp. His not-for-children children's book, *Dominoes*, was published in 2013. He has work forthcoming in *Blight Digest, Once Upon an Apocalypse Vol. I, Despumation Magazine*, and *Halloween Forevermore*. He has stunning muttonchops and a heart of gold.

Bracken MacLeod has worked as a martial arts teacher, a university philosophy instructor, for a children's non-profit, and as a criminal and civil trial attorney. In addition to *Shock Totem*, his short fiction has appeared in *Shotgun Honey, Sex and Murder Magazine, LampLight Magazine, Every Day Fiction, The Anthology: Year One* and *Year Two: Inner Demons Out, Reloaded: Both Barrels Vol. 2, Ominous Realities, The Big Adios,* and *Beat to a Pulp*. He has a story forthcoming in Issue 6 of the DIY horrorzine, *Splatterpunk*.

He is the author of the novel *Mountain Home*, and most recently a novella titled *White Knight* from **One Eye Press**.

He lives in New England and is currently at work on his next novel.

Night in the Forest of Loneliness

of Loneliness

by David G. Blake

She lured another one home. *Tightness expanded outward from her toes.* She told him her name was Willow, and he laughed and claimed his name was Oak. It was a fitting moniker; his laugh was wooden and his arms were unyielding limbs beneath her small hands. He kissed her, but she pushed him away and poured two glasses of wine. There may not have been a great deal of time left, but she still wanted to enjoy the process.

His green, leafy eyes twinkled mischievously as they drank. *Pain crawled from beneath her skin, from her feet upward to her calves.*

The wine was gone. The room rocked Willow to a swoon. *Numbness danced along her legs and caressed her thighs.* The sensation roused her and she found herself nestled in oaken limbs that swayed with the wind and whispered promises with every creak.

She considered asking him to leave, but her loneliness refused such a kindness. Her fingers unclasped each cold button of his shirt, and she pressed both palms against his hard chest, pushing him to the bed.

His green, lush eyes darkened with desire as she undressed. *Numbness pinched her nipples and waves of tantalizing pain rippled downward.*

The heat of wine bloomed down Willow's arms and into her fingertips. He gasped as she brushed them softly across his lips. *Pain raced beneath her skin, along her arms, and reached for him.* He pulled her closer and closed his eyes. The moist, intermingled warmth of their tongues exploded inward like rays of fattened sunshine. She breathed in the heat and exhaled it from every pore.

His green, dewy eyes misted with confusion. *Ripples in her skin hardened and tiny blooms ripped from her ovulating pores.*

Her fingernails pierced his skin and limbs curled from his mouth and nostrils. Bark swelled from between her thighs and tore into his navel. *Pain radiated in cycles of pleasure, each climax fueling the transformation.* Willow sunk her teeth into the flesh of his face and her tongue pollinated the wound. She growled with the voice of a tree snapping during a storm and grinded against him, arching toward the heat that was building around them.

His green, seedy eyes dilated as he screamed. *Warmth consumed both of them as roots ate through her skin and planted in the pollinated soil of his flesh.*

David G. Blake lives in Pennsylvania with his girlfriend and their chocolate lab. When he isn't trying to convince his girlfriend to let him buy an octopus, he spends his time trying to hack NASA's control systems so he can take Curiosity for a spin around Mars. In addition to *Shock Totem*, his work is forthcoming/has appeared in *Nature*, *Galaxy's Edge*, *Futures 2*, *Beneath Ceaseless Skies*, and many other publications.

Holiday Recollection

KORE

by John Langan

Annie, my wife, started the Halloween Walk when our son was three. We were renting a house on a quiet street. She'd learned that several of the kids in his preschool didn't go trick-or-treating because their neighborhoods weren't safe enough for their parents to take them out in. "We could do something, here," she said to me. "We could make a haunted walk for the kids behind the house." I agreed. Every kid should experience Halloween, right? Together, we set up a course for the kids that took them through the passage between the house and its garage, up the hill behind the garage, and along the terrace cut into the hill. We strung the cottony spider-webs we'd bought at Wal-Mart around the back passage, then populated them with our son's collection of rubber spiders; for a finishing touch, we hung his enormous tarantula puppet in the center of the alley, and told the kids they had to duck under it. We filled yellow dish-gloves with bubble wrap, dabbed streaks of red paint along the fingers, and jammed them into the wire fence that extended beyond the end of the garage. The paint dried pink, but the effect was more surreal than ludicrous. "Don't get caught by the hands of the dead," we said to the kids. At the other end of the terrace, on a white plastic chair, we sat the dummy we'd made from filling an old pair of my jeans and one of my old shirts with straw and tying the ends of the arms and legs closed. I had fashioned its head by turning a gallon milk-jug upside down and painting a green-skinned face on it. I'd given it large, baleful eyes. Annie placed half a watermelon that had slid past ripeness on the ground in front of the dummy, and jammed a dozen keys she'd bought at the dollar store into the liquescent fruit. This, we told the kids, was Frankenstein's monster. He was asleep, but might wake at any moment. His old, used-up brain was lying at his feet. Each of the kids had to poke around in his rotten gray matter until they found a key, which they had to extract without disturbing him.

Once everyone had a key, they had to run as fast as they could to the front of the house. There, Annie was waiting on the porch in an old-fashioned witch's costume (although the pointed hat was bright orange, its brim composed of netting). Each kid presented their key, which she inspected, then instructed them to drop into the plastic kettle before her. In exchange, the child received a brown paper lunch-bag decorated with spiders and skulls, and full of candy. After the last bag had been distributed, we escorted the kids up and down our street, where the trick-or-treating was plentiful and safe.

So big a hit was our first Halloween Walk that it became an instant tradition. A few years later, when we left that rental house to move to one we'd bought, there was a single question on the lips of our son's friends: "Are you still going to have Halloween in your new house?" Of course, we said. While smaller than our previous place, this house had a large, dry, mostly-empty basement. It was, Annie declared, the perfect place for the Walk. Once the sun had slid from the sky, I gathered our son and his friends at the back of the house, where the ground sloped steeply down, exposing the northeast corner of the basement and the door set there. Addressing the kids in the big, over-the-top voice of a circus ringmaster, I described what lay in store for them within. One year, it was Dr. Frankenstein's laboratory. Another, it was the halls in which Dr. Moreau kept his worst experiments confined. A third time, it was the caverns under Count Dracula's (supposedly) abandoned castle. As with that first Walk, each journey presented a goal for the kids to accomplish. They had to steal the batteries Dr. Frankenstein intended to power his next monstrous creation. They had to rescue the (stuffed) animals slated for Dr. Moreau's forthcoming round of vivisection. They had to locate and retrieve the magic rings that would permit Dracula to be resurrected. Flashlight in hand, I led them counter-clockwise around the basement, directing the light at mason jars stuffed with rubber eyeballs, at buckets brimming with plastic snakes, at cryptic graffiti on the cement walls. Our destination was always the same: the small room off the southeast corner of the basement. When the real estate agent had shown us the house, she had described the space as a sauna. There was an improvised metal basket full of large, round stones across from the door, so it seemed possible the room had been used for steam. But the open drain in the center of the floor had looked wider than what you would have expected in a sauna. It was deep, too, beyond the range of the flashlight we shone into it. Some kind of drywell, we decided, and covered it with a square of plywood. As I led the kids into the room, I positioned myself at the cover, to keep them clear of it. After the group had fulfilled its annual task, I sent the kids upstairs, where Annie, in some variation of a witch's costume (but always with that orange hat), was waiting for them with bags of candy.

This past Halloween was our most elaborate, yet. We had settled on an archaeological theme, Indiana Jones meets the Mummy, so to speak. There was a big bag of sand left over from one of the aquariums; we scattered it over the floor. We placed plastic snakes, rubber spiders and scorpions, around the room. I chalked the most sinister hieroglyphs I could find online onto the basement walls. A friend provided us with a six-foot cardboard box that I spray painted gold then hand painted a pharaoh's mannered features onto. We propped our handmade sarcophagus against one side of the sauna and strewed plastic human bones about the floor. For the first time, I incorporated the drywell into the night's events, removing the cover and filling the floor surrounding it with more malevolent sigils. Also for the first time, Annie took a more active role in the actual Walk. About a month before Halloween, we had attended a birthday party for one of our son's friends. The party had had a classical mythology theme, and had climaxed with the gathered party-goers taking turns smashing a huge piñata in the shape of Medusa's head. The rubber snakes with which the piñata was adorned flew off during the attempts to open it, but the head itself was largely intact, and Annie, already thinking ahead, had asked our hosts if she could take it home. "What for?" I'd asked. "You'll see," she'd answered. By trimming the ragged opening at the base of the neck, she transformed it into an oversized mask. She added a pair of long, gray gloves and a pale green gown she'd picked up at the Salvation Army, and *voilà*, she was a goddess. "Which goddess?" I said. "That's not important," she said. Her plan was to sit in the corner of the sauna opposite the sarcophagus. The kids would see the mask and assume it was just another prop; when she stood, it would scare the bejeezus out of them. "What if we use the drywell?" I said. "What if the kids have to throw something into it in order to propitiate you?" "Not me," she said, "the goddess." But we agreed that I would give them each a piece of bite-sized candy that they would have to drop into the well to appease the goddess.

By and large, the Halloween Walk went well. I was concerned that our son and his friends, all of whom are around eleven, might be too old for another Walk, that our props might be too amateurish for them, but both our son and a couple of his friends bought into the scenario with real gusto, which helped to sell it to the rest of the kids. Even the boy who kept insisting that he wasn't afraid of any of this, it was all so *fake*, was looking fairly unsettled. And when I had them gathered in the sauna, which I re-christened the Chamber of Souls, and Annie slowly rose from her seat, the kids gave a collective gasp. "It's Robbie's mom," someone whispered. "Is it?" someone else replied. Playing along, our son said, "That doesn't look like my mom." "She's in a costume—duh!" the first kid hissed. "My mom's upstairs," our son said, managing to sound genuinely nervous. For all its simplicity, I suppose the costume was effective—maybe because of its simplicity. The face on the oversized head was stylized, more department-store mannequin than classical portrait. Its blank eyes were too large for the other features, the narrow, almost pointed nose, the pouting lips. The left cheek was wrinkled, a memento of its previous existence as a piñata. Annie held her head at such an angle that those empty eyes seemed to stare at a point directly above the kids' heads. "Oh Ancient Power," I said, "we bring offerings for your honor. Accept them, and do not drag us down to the darkness where you reign." Considering it was improvised pretty much on the spot, I thought my supplication sounded pretty good. Two and three at a time, the kids darted forward and flung the pieces of candy I gave them into the drywell. A couple of the girls shrieked as they did. The resident skeptic tossed his Hershey's Kiss into the hole with a motion that was probably intended to be dismissive but that came across as full of dread. (I'll admit, I was more pleased by that than I should have been.)

The only part of the Walk that didn't go according to plan involved the younger brother of one of son's friends. He was seven, and a particularly wide-eyed and tremulous seven at that. I wasn't sure that the Walk would be appropriate for him, but he insisted with all of a younger brother's desire not to be left out of his older brother's fun that he wanted to take part in it. His mother offered to accompany us, which I thought would reassure him should he find anything too intense. For most of the Walk, I was right. While I elaborated the terrible history of the latest stop on our tour, I heard the boy's mother murmuring to him, and while his eyes retained their shocked expression, he appeared to be tolerating the event. However, when it came his turn to step out and add his candy to those already cast into the drywell, he refused. "Come on," his mother said lightly, "it's no big deal." The boy shook his head violently. In fact, his entire body was trembling, as if he were freezing. "Come on," his mother said, "it's just Ms. Annie." That loosened his tongue. Through chattering teeth, he said, "How do you know?" "What do you mean?" his mother said. "How do you *know*?" he said. "*How do you know?*" I half-expected Annie to remove her mask, show the boy that his mother was right, it was only her, but she remained still. "*How do you know?*" the boy said over his mother's calm insistence that this was all a game, we were just playing, it was Halloween and that was Ms. Annie in her costume. "*How do you know?*" Finally, I stepped in and announced that it was time for the kids to go upstairs, to receive their bags of candy. I herded my son and his friends to the staircase, cautioning them to watch their steps. As soon as my son opened the door to the kitchen, lighting the stairs, I turned back towards the sauna. But the younger boy and his mom were already on their way out of it, and although his eyes were still wet with tears, he appeared more embarrassed than frightened. Nonetheless, I stopped to talk with his mom, who assured me her son was fine. "Your wife," she said, "is some actress. She had me creeped out." "Me too," I laughed. I ducked my head into the sauna to check for Annie, but she had already left, exiting the basement door to circle around the front of the house and in the front door. By the time I climbed to the kitchen door, she was in the midst of the kids, dressed in her usual witch's costume, this one consisting of a plain black dress the ends of whose sleeves and skirt had been pre-cut to appear ragged, a heavy necklace, and the orange hat. I wound my way through the kids to where she was pouring cups of apple cider and kissed her on the back of the neck. "You are something," I said. "You have no idea," she said, and passed me a cup to hand to one of our son's friends.

It's strange how quickly such an event recedes into your memory. Not until a month later, the weekend after Thanksgiving, did I think about it again in any kind of detail. It was late Saturday night—early Sunday morning, technically. I clawed my way out of the thick folds of a sleep that had wrapped around me like a blanket. I wasn't certain what had awakened me. To be honest, I had the sense that it was because I'd been so profoundly asleep that I'd woken, as if my body had dragged me back into myself from some other state. There was something different about the house. It was like when the power goes out while you've been asleep and you wake to the air colder, the chorus of noises that fills the nighttime hours silent. I glanced to my left, but Annie's side of the bed was empty. Was that what I'd registered, her rising to visit the bathroom? I listened for the sound of her moving downstairs but didn't hear anything. Of course, she might have retreated to the guest room futon to escape my snoring. Only when I was rolling over to return to sleep did I register the figure standing in the corner of the room, to the right of the door. Instantly, I was sitting upright, my heart hammering as if I'd been doused with a bucket of freezing water. The shadows were particularly thick where the form was, away from the windows, but I could make out the oversized head, the dress. I opened my mouth to say, "Honey?" but stopped, overwhelmed by the certainty that, whoever was in the room with me, it was not Annie. For what couldn't have been as long as it seemed, the figure stood in place, its head tilted towards me, while I sat where I was, that little boy's question looping in my mind ("*How do you know?*"). The darkness seemed grainier in that part of the room, as if the air were different, somehow; I had the impression of tremendous distance and age. At last, the figure turned to its right and walked out the door. I waited for the stairs to the living room to utter their creaks and groans, but they remained mute. There was nothing I wanted to do less than leave the bed to see what had become of the intruder. But my son was asleep in his room, and my wife was somewhere else in the house. With as much stealth as I could muster, I slid out from between the sheets and padded to the door, regretting that I'd never gotten around to hiding that baseball bat under the bed. The landing outside the room was empty. My son's door was shut. I opened it, anyway, to check on him, but he was soundly asleep, unaccompanied by any weird visitors. Could the figure have descended the staircase in silence? It seemed unlikely, yet appeared the only possibility. I followed it down, my heavy footsteps announcing my passage. The first floor was empty of both the intruder and Annie. At this, I felt a momentary surge of panic, and, sliding one of the long knives from the butcher block beside the coffee maker, headed for the basement stairs.

I found Annie in the sauna, crouched over the drywell. She was naked, her hair hanging down around her face. She'd preserved the hieroglyphs I'd drawn on the floor around the hole, and added a few of her own. In her right hand, she held an assortment of candies. With her left, she was picking them up one at a time and casting them into the well. I set the knife on the floor beside the door and walked toward her. I didn't know what to say. Without looking up, without speaking, she held out a candy to me. I took it. It was a bite-sized Charleston Chew. I'd lost a tooth to one of these when I was a kid. The tooth had been loose but not that loose, and had torn free of the gum with a sweet, sharp pain that had flooded my mouth with the taste of blood and sugar. I gazed at the drywell, at the circle of blackness that dropped who knew how far to who knew what destination. "You have no idea," Annie had said to me Halloween night. I didn't. I tossed my offering into the darkness, and reached to my wife for the next one.

For Fiona

Out of Field Theory

by Kevin Lucia

Brian Palmer shivered despite the noonday sun warming his shoulders. "This is it," he muttered, staring at the picture he'd just taken. "Holy shit...I think this is it. This picture is going to change my fucking *life*. This. Is. *It*."

About time. He'd flipped through all the pictures he'd taken so far with his Nikon 351 Digital Camera and not one of them had been worth a damn. The first one had been fuzzy, out of focus. Couldn't see that barn on Bassler Road for shit. Another had been framed wrong, cutting the top off the old gazebo in the abandoned koi garden down the road. The brilliant yellow and orange koi swimming in the old pond next to the gazebo? Red and yellow blobs.

And some of the other shots he'd taken? Of Bassler Road curving into the wooded distance at sunset? Of an abandoned old truck sitting by the railroad tracks? He liked them okay, but he knew what Professor

Spinella would say: they looked like stock photos in Adirondack guidebooks found in tourist-trap novelty stores everywhere.

That wouldn't cut it if he wanted his final project for Photography Philosophy to pass. He needed something unique that he could examine through a philosophy they'd studied this semester, philosophies he'd had a hard enough time understanding from the start.

But as he'd flipped through more of the pictures he'd taken that morning; of the water flowing under Black Creek Bridge. The abandoned factory on Black River along Route 28 toward Whitelake. Several angles of the unused bandstand next to Raedeker Park Zoo, he'd realized glumly that every. single. picture. *sucked*.

Except this one.

Brian's frustrated thoughts had screeched to a halt at the sight of it, something in the photo catching his eye. He'd taken the picture only a few minutes ago, of an old Victorian farmhouse out in the middle of a fallow cornfield off Bassler Road. On a whim, he'd zoomed in on the front door and the window next to it, then snapped the shot, not thinking much about it.

But upon review, he'd created a striking effect. The area around the doorway had endured the years passingly well, but damp rot riddled the siding around the window, and the rot looked as if it was spreading toward the door. Like a rash infecting healthy tissue.

"Jeez," he muttered, tapping the zoom button. "That's actually not bad. In fact, it's..."

He trailed off.

In the window, at the very edge of the image's frame...something. A smudge. A shadow. Of...

Of what, he couldn't tell, because his framing had cut off the rest.

Brian looked over his shoulder back at the old house, thinking. Dimly, he remembered a framing theory they'd studied in class this year, developed by some guy named Deleuze. Something about how a picture was framed...

He raised the camera and looked at the image again, at the cut-off shadow in the window. Though not word for word, he recalled a snippet from an essay written by

Deleuze, assigned to his class early in the semester:

...the out of field phenomenon occurs when literal framing of an image leaves elements and actions partly out of frame, implying their continuation past the frame...

The philosophy part of Photography Philosophy had been rough going. The class was less about *how* to take pictures, more about *why* people should take pictures. Brian hadn't understood much of it. He liked taking pictures of interesting things. Who cared *why*?

Like the rest of the philosophy they'd studied the past semester, he'd struggled to understand Deleuze's ideas. However, something about the guy's out-of-field-theory had stuck with Brian, even if he *hadn't* gotten all of the guy's philosophies completely.

Professor Spinella had explained it this way: anything cut off by the framing of a picture didn't actually end, but rather continued outside the frame somewhere else, because photographing images created another reality, a reality of the image, which wasn't limited by the artificial framing imposed by the photographic device. He'd thought the whole thing a bunch of mumbo jumbo when they'd first studied it, but...

He tapped the image on the Nikon's small screen, his stomach tingling with excitement. Maybe he'd found at least *one* photo that would pass muster with Spinella and help him earn him a passing grade on his final project. Maybe he could take some more shots of this house and use them for a presentation of Deleuze's theory.

He glanced at his watch: 2:00 PM. Plenty of time for him to take some more pictures, maybe even jimmy his way inside, see if he could find something interesting to shoot. And he should be able to get enough pictures before it got dark. Because who wanted to muck around an old house after dark, right?

He slipped his hand into a small satchel slung over his shoulder, digging for another memory card he could use for the camera, intent on filling the whole thing with pictures of this house. The prospect of actually taking pictures that *meant* something to him, for a change, was exciting.

Just so long as he got his ass out of there

before dark.

* * *

A year ago as a senior in high school, when his entry of a sunset over Blue Mountain Lake won first prize in Old Forge Academy's Harper Penny Photography Scholarship Contest, Brian never imagined he'd be so desperate to take a "unique" photograph. Everyone liked his pictures back then. His parents had indulged his hobby, sacrificing their meager savings to buy him his Nikon for his 16th birthday. He'd served as president of Old Forge Academy's Photo Club for three years straight. Was one of the lead photographers for the school journal and yearbook. The summer before and after his senior year, he'd done some freelance work for the Webb County Courier (paid in contributor copies only, but a byline was a byline.) The scholarship he'd won enabled him to attend Webb Community College to study Photography, assuring him (in his mind, anyway) of a successful career behind the viewfinder.

But only a year into his studies had given Brian a new, depressing perspective. Though he "freelanced" for the campus newspaper, his photos were hardly ever used, apparently not "fresh" or "original" enough. His old spot with the Courier had been handed over to a high school successor. He'd eagerly tramped through the countryside all summer after graduation, taking scenic pictures of waterfalls, creeks, lakes, old cabins, mountains...hell, even sunsets, submitting them to every contest and journal he could find, confident of his success simply because he could now list "Photography Major at Webb Community College" in his bio.

All his photos had been rejected by form letters stating: "Thank you for your interest but at this time, your photos don't meet our needs. Please submit again in the future."

Soon as his classes started and the semester wore on, his studies and various class projects ate into his free time, cutting his own personal photography into a third of what it was. Complicating matters: his scholarship paid for tuition, room and board, and a limited meal plan. Gas money, grocery money, laundromat money, book money, photo supplies...he was on his own. His father worked construction, his mother was a part-time nurse. They just met their own needs, so he expected little to no extra money from home.

So, he reluctantly found work as a checkout-bagger at The Great American Grocery down the road from campus. Working nearly twenty-five hours a week there, on top of his schoolwork, left very little time to actually take pictures for himself.

Brian stopped about five feet from the old house's front door, wrestling as always with his future, his dreams, and their slow, painful death this past year. It would be incredibly convenient to claim that his brand of traditional photography wasn't accepted in a digital world in which images could be so easily enhanced. He could blame his mediocre grades on how tight his schedule was. He always felt so tired, unable to focus. All the ideas in his head seemed breathtaking when day-dreaming at work, but when he had the rare moment to actually get behind his camera, the results seldom matched his expectations anymore.

His professors, so far, had felt the same way. Best he'd managed in any of his classes the past year was a B. He could say that was because of work, or not having enough time to develop his technique. The truth of the matter? In his gut knew that none of his excuses were valid. Several of his classmates were only carrying B averages, but their photos possessed something his lacked.

His fellow students' photos had a kind of shine, a vitality, while his photos looked like flat, lifeless things, even to his eyes.

He supposed it was the same with acting and writing. A really bad actor, you could *see* how hard they were acting. A bad writer, all you saw were words strung together that tried too hard to *tell* a story, not capture a reader *in* a story.

Everything he'd shot over the last year had been the same. You could see all the different angles and focuses and lighting techniques he'd learned, like a goddamn checklist. But, when viewed at as a whole...

His photos fell flat. Didn't at all match the visions in his head. They had no life of their own.

The truth of the matter, then, was far simpler, and a lot more depressing. He had just enough talent to turn photography into a nice hobby, if he pursued it...and that was it.

That picture he'd taken, however.

Something different about it. A vibe, a tenor he'd not sensed in his work thus far. If the image he'd just shot of this old house hadn't be a fluke, if he could take more like that...maybe his dreams weren't dead, after all.

He paused before stepping forward, checking the batteries on his Nikon, wondering about the history of the place. He wasn't a Clifton Heights native. His cousin Rich lived here, had suggested a month ago that Clifton Heights would be a good place to take pictures. Said it was a "unique" town, "kinda scenic'n shit." When he saw Rich again, he'd have to ask him about the history of this old place.

Satisfied with the camera's battery levels, Brian approached the front door. Whatever its history, the house felt long abandoned.

Like no one had lived in it for years. Decades, maybe.

Brian stopped several paces from the crumbling remains of the house's front porch. There it stood, tottering, like every abandoned house he'd ever seen. Paint largely peeled away, several windows without glass, roof sagging in places. He imagined it had once been a stately old home, almost like a manor or something.

His gaze traveled over the decayed face of the house. As he settled on the window and door he'd snapped a picture of, an uneasy thought occurred to him: that shadow. In his excitement over the picture's resonance he'd never considered what had thrown the shadow.

A brief chill passed through him.

He shivered, but shook it off. There hadn't been a real shadow there, of course. An angle of the light was all, something formed in the "reality" created by his camera, nothing more. In fact...that sounded like an excellent lead-in for his project, that the shadow had been created by his framing, created by the reality *he* had created in his taking the picture.

Bolstered by this idea, he strode forward. As he neared the front door, he saw (with just the faintest relief) that indeed, no shadow loomed in the window. *C'mon. You want to be a photographer? For real? Suck it up, Nancy.*

He placed a hand on the door, pushed it open, and stepped inside.

• • •

A foul odor assaulted his nose as he entered what remained of the home's foyer. Brittle wallpaper flaked away from the walls. Grit crunched beneath his shoes. For some reason, he hadn't expected such a rotten smell...but of course it made sense. Empty for years, no one living in it, heating it or taking care of it, everything moldering in the wet and the damp, freezing through winter ice only to thaw into rot again every Spring. Probably nothing here had escaped it. He realized if this house had a basement or even a crawlspace beneath the floor, he'd need to be wary of his footing.

Also, the dark. Not pitch black, but

definitely something he needed to account for. He held up his camera, toggled to "lighting options" on the digital menu and selected "night portrait," adjusting the flash settings for optimal exposure...

Something scuttled across the floor, from left to right.

Brian stiffened, goose-flesh rippling across his skin. Adrenaline surged and his heart pounded...

And he instantly felt stupid, though his heart still thumped and it took considerable effort to shake off his jangling nerves. A mouse. A squirrel, a chipmunk, or God forbid...even a rat. Only a rodent of some kind that his heavy footsteps had sent scurrying for cover. Place was probably lousy with them, and he didn't need to be...

His eyes focused on the hallway before him, which receded to the back of the house. Clearly the main hall, which opened up into a large room in the rear. A den, or perhaps a dining room. Off the hall on both sides, several doors led to other rooms, and as he stared down that hall...something *clicked* in his head. A switch *flipped*. Possessed by an inspiration he'd not felt all year, Brian raised his Nikon, focused on the hallway, stepped sideways so that his framing caught the hallway at an angle, partially cutting off its opening...

He snapped a picture.

And in the flash, his fancy took over. Replacing the rotten walls with wallpaper, installing polished wooden floors and a stucco ceiling. In the camera's flash, his mind conjured what this room must've looked like years before.

The image faded.

Replaced by the damp, moldy reality of now. But a feverish excitement filled him (tinged by the faint worry that, like always, the finished product wouldn't match his imagination) as he thought how he could use these photos for his final project. Filled with enthusiasm, Brian gave himself over to the camera as he hadn't since high school, losing himself in the process as he moved and shot, moved and shot, his eye becoming the camera, his mind using the camera's flash to wash away the decay with images conjured from his imagination of what might have been before time and the elements ravaged the walls of this house.

* * *

Sometime later Brian returned to himself. Dazed, breathing heavily, clutching his Nikon as if his life depended on it. He took a deep, steadying breath and blinked his eyes. Suddenly aware of the room's chill and the sweat gluing his shirt to his chest, he shivered and looked around.

Sunlight filtered in through a smudged, gritty window. Leftover furniture—recliners, kitchen chairs, end tables—had been stacked carelessly around the room. The fabric of the recliners in tatters, the end tables and kitchen tables in rotten pieces. Also, wooden crates had been stacked against the wall, full of unidentifiable—

His jumbled thoughts seized as he came upon a yawning black rectangle. A doorway. Whatever door had once been there was long since gone. The walls surrounding the door were made of cinder-block, its gray surface splotched with black-green mold.

He had no way of knowing, but he didn't think that door led to another room. The darkness beyond looked thick and absolute. A dank and cold earthen smell wafted from it. *Basement*, his mind whispered. *Maybe root cellar*.

He lowered the Nikon, closed his eyes and rubbed his temples with his fingertips. How long had he been in the zone?

He'd shot "in the zone" before, of course...though not since high school. He supposed other creative types experienced something similar. At a peak moment of creative excitement, the conscious mind fades while intuition takes over. Used to happen to him a lot. When he was shooting woodland trails, lakes, mountains, sporting events in high school, he'd slipped into the "zone" without noticing, just pointing and shooting, pointing and shooting, almost unconsciously framing shots he thought looked good. And when he reviewed his shots after coming out of the zone, they *were* good (they'd always looked good back then) and many of them he didn't remember taking at all, so deeply immersed he'd been.

But going into the zone had never felt like this. Back then he'd slipped in and out of the zone, smooth as silk. This, with his heart pounding, breathing as if he'd run a marathon, sweating rivers...

He felt like he'd been *sucked* into the zone...and almost hadn't made it back out again.

He held up his Nikon with trembling fingers. How many pictures had he taken?

He looked at the digital screen, which showed the looming black doorway to the basement, but also, in the right bottom corner, a little red 15. Fifteen pictures. He'd taken only fifteen pictures, though it felt more like fifty.

The next question: fifteen pictures of what? Like always, when "in the zone," he couldn't really remember *what* he'd taken pictures of. As his thumb hovered over the *review* toggle, a strange compulsion gripped him: *delete them all.* He should go back to the main menu, select Batch Delete, wipe the whole memory card clean, and get the hell out of here.

On the heels of that thought, rationality

kicked in, sneering. *Why? It's only an old, rundown house.*

And with that thought, he pressed *review*. A spread of thumbnail images replaced the basement door on the Nikon's screen, the first thumbnail outlined in yellow. He pressed *review* again, bringing up the first image.

He had to squint at first to make out anything, because not only was the back room dim...

Why aren't you looking at these outside?

...but the room in the image was, like much of the rest of the house, badly damaged by damp rot, the wallpaper blackened with water damage. No furniture was readily apparent in this shot...

There.

In the corner, mostly out of frame. A head...a horse's head? With a handle sticking from its cheek. A rocking horse. A child's room?

He peered closer. Couldn't see the rest of the rocking horse because it was mostly out of frame, but he figured it looked like most rocking horses...

He sucked in a deep breath.

A shadow.

Like the one in the window, from his first picture. A shadow above and behind the rocking horse's head, also mostly cut off by his framing, but from this angle, it looked like...

The shadow...

Was riding the rocking horse.

His sweat-damp t-shirt suddenly felt ice-cold, and he shivered. A handful of feeble explanations offered themselves, but most of them fell flat, if only because he now dimly recalled the window in that room facing *away* from the sun. No light streaming through that window, throwing his or some other shadow on the wall behind the rocking horse.

What was it, then?

Nothing. An odd coloration of the wall. A smudge on the lens. Nothing. But he quickly dismissed the notion of hitting the zoom and looking closer, to see if the shadow extended over the handle on the rocking horse's head, forming the barest suggestion of fingers. He toggled to the next picture, instead.

Why aren't you looking at these outside?

The room in the next image was more easily identifiable, if only because of the bookshelves—warped, crooked, several shelves broken—and what looked like an old rocking chair in the far left corner, also mostly cut out of frame. A sitting room of sorts. There was probably more bookshelves out of frame, maybe a table and a few recliners.

He zoomed in on the bookshelves, a cautious admiration replacing his uneasiness. It was a stirring shot of books—knowledge, understanding, intellect—destroyed by something so basic as time and the elements. Some of the books looked intact, while others looked swollen with damp-rot, pages likely stuck together, ink smudged and unreadable. This was a *good* picture. He could already imagine the narration for it (a whole bit about time and nature succeeding knowledge) in his final project.

"Hell yeah," he whispered as he panned left, "in the zone again, finally...

"*Shit!*"

A streak of ice raced down his back,

arrowed straight to his guts. His fingers failed. His precious Nikon tumbled from his fingers and landed with a dull *thud* at his feet. He blinked, and in a flash, he thought he saw the same thing he'd just seen in the camera floating in the yawning blackness of the basement door.

His neck tingled. His stomach gurgled, his heart pounding to sudden frantic life in his chest. He closed his eyes and counted to ten, squeezing his hands into fists so tightly his knuckles ached and his fingernails bit into his palms.

"Nothing," he rasped, his voice sounding thin and insubstantial in the suddenly heavy and oppressive silence. "Nothing there."

After a ten count, he swallowed and opened his eyes, looking into the emptiness of the basement doorway...

Nothing.

Except impenetrable darkness. But the ice still rippled across his shoulders and down his back. His heart still pounded away. Slowly, he knelt and picked up his Nikon, without taking his eyes off the black doorway. He stood, thought about turning and striding out of that back room, but opted instead for backpedaling, slowly, as if afraid of giving his back to that doorway, as if afraid of...waking something up.

Which was stupid and ridiculous.

There was likely nothing in that basement or root cellar or whatever except mold and cobwebs and spiders, maybe a few garter snakes or rats. No ghostly face— which he thought he'd seen sitting in that rocking chair, peeking around the edge of the frame—was going to float out of that dark basement doorway any time soon.

so long as you keep an eye on it and don't turn your back on it

Stupid.

But he didn't look back down at the picture of the drawing room, just toggled ahead to the next picture, some distant part of his brain yammering, *Why are you still here?*

Hands shaking, he raised the Nikon, glancing from the Nikon's screen to the empty basement doorway and back again, still back-pedaling, until his back thumped against the door-frame to the room, causing him to jump. He shifted, stepped backward out of the room, and suddenly (to his slight shame) he spun around, scrambling for the door like a man fleeing a live hand grenade. His fingers grasped the soft, rotten edge of the door and he slammed it shut.

He stepped away, telling himself that *no*, he hadn't seen an indistinct darkness rushing from the black well of the basement across the room after him, and no, the doorknob of the door did *not* jiggle for an instant, that was just a residual vibration of him slamming it shut.

Even so, he felt much better with that door between him and the yawning black basement doorway. Because shadows couldn't grasp and turn doorknobs could they?

but they can seep under doors

He shook off the foolish thought. Dammit, he was *finally*, after a year of frustration and dead ends, taking *damn* good pictures. He wasn't about to let a stupid case of the willies ruin that. And, as if in defiance of this, he ignored the bottom of that door...

which shadows very well could *seep under*

...held up the Nikon and looked at the

next picture.

A trembling sigh of relief escaped his lips. This was a picture of the kitchen, what remained of it. He'd framed what looked like the sink area, everything covered in a thick layer of dirt and grime. As he examined the photo, his fears subsided, a running narration in his head (for his project) detailing about how much of everyday life had most likely centered around this now abandoned and desolate kitchen sink: washing hands before dinner, washing dishes after dinner, getting a cool drink of water on a hot summer day...

His gaze slipped to the bottom left-hand corner of the image. He squinted and, feeling none of the fear he'd felt only moments ago, zoomed in on the bottom-left hand corner.

Looked like something triangular and metal—an ax? He couldn't tell, but it looked as if someone had, with a mighty swing, lodged an ax in the counter-top's edge...

an ax someone had once used to do horrible, horrible things

He shook his head, closed his eyes and pinched the bridge of his nose. "Jeez. I'm goin buggy. I gotta get out of here and get home."

When he opened his eyes and turned to do just that, he noticed two things that brought his gooseflesh rippling back.

One: it was getting dark, harder to see. How late was it?

Two: he didn't recognize the room he stood in at all. Empty, floor littered and gritty, wallpaper moldy, doorways stood to his left, right, and before him. The door to the backroom and the basement directly behind him.

And, maybe it was a trick of the fading light, but he couldn't see very far down either of the halls. Which was crazy, of course. How big could the house be?

He swallowed down a cresting hysteria, cracking his neck. It was only a big old rambling farmhouse. Didn't matter which hall he took, it would eventually lead back to the front door, right?

But still, he couldn't make himself step toward either of the three halls. Grunting in what felt like vain, childish defiance, he raised the Nikon and toggled to the next picture. Maybe there'd be a landmark he'd recognize, some image that might jog his memory about which hallway he should take...

out of frame, you're out of frame and never coming back

"Fuck that shit," he said, more of a whine than growl. He held up the Nikon and looked at the image.

The bathroom.

He'd centered this shot on the toilet. The sink next to it and the mirror above the sink just peeked into view, cut off at the frame's edge...

He opened his mouth. To swear, to gasp, he wasn't sure, except he suddenly struggled for the breath to do any of those things. In the mirror, slipping off the frame's edge...

A shadow.

Like the one in the outside window.

what lies cut off by the frame still continues off the frame in a reality created by the photographic device

He cleared his throat and said in a voice more quavery than defiant, "That's it. I gotta get the fuck *outta* this place."

But which direction? Which hallway? He could keep paging through the rest of these photos...

but he didn't want to because he thought maybe in each one the shadow of the thing hiding just past the frame would get closer and closer

...but he didn't think looking at those pictures would help him one damn bit in remembering the way out. And then, it hit him with the force of lightning: the back room. Where that empty basement door was...

and the shadow rushing across the room

He'd seen trees outside the one window. Past that room was the outside. Maybe he could jimmy the window open, crawl through it, get out that way?

Maybe. Just maybe. Problem was...he'd have to face that basement door, again...and whatever was waiting in the darkness below...

click

click-click-clickity-click

Icy fear flushed down his spine. The doorknob. In the door leading to the backroom. Something was jiggling the doorknob on the other side.

Bullshit. It was something else, had to

be...

But as he forced himself to look over his shoulder, he caught a glimpse of the doorknob turning all the way with a final-sounding *click*...

And the door cracked open.

Fuck this!

Brian plunged forward, sprinting down the hall directly ahead. His feet pounded on the old wooden floors, sounding strangely hollow and dull, seeming to underscore how alone he was, and that there was no one to hear or to help him...

something crackled across the floor after him, like crisp autumn leaves skittering on concrete

He pumped his arms and ran harder than he ever had, and yet, impossibly, the end of the hall never came. As if he were running on a treadmill, the room ahead never seemed to get closer, and countless, innumerable open doors to infinite rooms flashed by, and he couldn't help seeing from the corner of his eye...

shadows rushing toward him
lying on beds

dangling in nooses from crossbeams
swinging axes
dancing, flitting, cavorting
rocking on wooden horses and sitting in chairs
lying in bathtubs

Shadows spun and twisted in those rooms while Brian pounded down that never-ending hallway, his breath roaring in his ears, his lungs aching as a stitch burned in his side. God, he wasn't going to make it and the cold behind him was rushing closer...

With an explosion of breath, like a drowning swimmer finally bursting to the surface, Brian launched through the doorway at the end. He whirled, grabbing frantically at the door. In his desperation, his sweaty hands slipped on the old brass knob as something skittered and hissed down the hall...

His fingers closed on the knob.

He glimpsed something like wide black eyes and a wrinkled, snarling mouth rushing toward him.

And he slammed the door shut.

Silence.

Save his panting and wheezing and a

high-pitched keening sound which, as he backed away from the door, he realized came from him.

He breathed air in giant, sobbing gulps, backing away from the door. "Shit. Shit, shit, shit, whatthefuckisthis. Gotta get outta here."

He spun, eyes frantically tracking the room. It looked like a den. Old, unused fireplace against the far wall. Three sagging couches facing the fireplace, what was probably an ornamental rug on the floor between them. In the far left corner, a door. To his immediate right, a staircase curving away to a second landing. To his immediate left...

Yes.

The foyer.

He recognized this room now. He'd started here, though that didn't make any sense at all, because he distinctly remembered a hall leading to many rooms, not a den like this, but he didn't care because there was the foyer and past that the front door...

His relief morphed instantly to panic as his shoulder thumped against a door that wouldn't open. The doorknob clicked uselessly in his hand. No matter how hard he twisted or turned it, laid his shoulder against the door, it remained closed.

Locked?

No, idiot. Stuck. Old house warped by rain and cold and sun. It's jammed, is all.

But the window. The front window. The very first picture he'd taken was of the front door and the window next to it. He rounded the corner of the foyer to the window, grabbed at its latches with trembling fingers, yanked upward....

Nothing.

He saw the catch, saw it was still locked. Cursing his stupidity, he fumbled with the catch, trying to flip it over...

Frozen. With rust and time. The window-frame was also probably warped out of true, just like the door.

"No problem, right?" he muttered. "It's glass. We can break that shit."

He glanced around. There, on the floor near one of the couches, unbelievably enough an old flashlight, one of the heavy, metal ones. Proof others folks had been in here besides him, right?

but why is it still here why leave the flashlight here?

He ignored the shaking voice clamoring in his brain. Scrambled over to the flashlight and scooped it up. For some reason, the cool, metal tube felt reassuring in his hand. He leaped toward the window, winding the flashlight up...

A bright flash stabbed his eyes. The sun? Coming through the glass at just the right moment, blinding him?

"Jeez! Shit!" Brian's aborted swing fell short as he clapped his other hand on his eyes, rubbing them. His vision wavered and blurred, out of focus. He rubbed them harder. Stepped closer to the window, looked down the drive...

And for a minute, his heart skipped.

Like an engine run too hard for too long, his mind threw several gears as a black emptiness yawned beneath his feet.

The old flashlight fell with a hollow thud from nerveless fingers.

Outside.

Someone standing down the drive

toward Bassler Road, their...*his*...back to him. Seeming to be considering something in his hands.

Brian gaped. A fish on land, drowning in air, as he raked trembling fingers through his hair, pulling on tufts, pulling *hard*, trying to make himself wake up...

The person at the end of the drive turned suddenly, appraising the house with what looked like intense interest and excitement...

Holding in his hands a NIKON 351.

Brian rasped shallow, hitching breaths. He sagged against the window, hands pressed flat against the cold glass. The figure at the end of the drive held up his Nikon, presumably examining pictures they'd just taken...of the front door and window in juxtaposition, of course.

Brian slowly backed away from the window, legs quivering, made of boneless jelly. All his will and energy leaked out of him and it took every ounce of reserve left in him not to collapse into a huddled pile on the dusty floor.

The shadow.

The shadow in the window. The shadow

he'd seen in his picture. That shadow was...

It was...

The door to his left—the one he'd slammed shut on that rushing dark—rocked in its frame. The door knob jiggled once. The door creaked.

Fell still.

And slammed open. Something dark and vaporous with cold teeth rushed into the room. There was nowhere left to run and Brian threw up his arms and screamed as an ice cold filled him...

• • •

Brian Palmer shivered.

"This is it," he muttered, staring at the picture he'd just taken. "Holy shit...I think this is it. This is going to change my fucking *life*."

Kevin Lucia is an Associate Fiction Editor for *The Horror Channel*. His short fiction has appeared in several anthologies, and he's the author of *Things Slip Through* and *Devourer of Souls*. He's currently finishing his Creative Writing Masters Degree at Binghamton University. He teaches high school English and lives in Castle Creek, New York, with his wife and children.

TRICKS AND TREATS

by Rose Blackthorn

Wouldn't you rather just find a party? Or we could get a scary movie, and watch it at my house." Samantha, who went by Sam, pulled on the dangling laces of her sweatpants nervously. Something to keep her hands busy.

"Hey, they got the candy for free by begging door to door. It's not like it's really stealing." Cash went through another box in the cluttered garage, looking for something. His long hair was dark and kind of greasy, which went well with his oil-stained jeans and faded rock t-shirt. "Ah ha!" With a flourish, he pulled a dirty battered hockey mask from a pile of junk. "Perfect."

Sam sighed, fingers fumbling with her drawstring. Hijacking little kids for their candy was not the way she'd hoped to spend this Halloween.

"You still have any of your old costumes? Best bet is to cover your face, just to be safe." Cash put the hockey mask in place, and tied the string behind his head that would keep it there. His eyes, a vivid shade of blue like a clear sky in autumn, showed through the holes of the mask. With the rest of his expression hidden, he could have been anyone. "Come on, Sam. It'll be dark in half an hour. Then we can start harvesting our own haul of candy."

"Maybe you should just go trick-or-treating yourself." She had been looking forward to tonight for a month, but her imaginings had included going through the local haunted house attraction, maybe holding hands in the dark while she pretended to be scared. She'd even gone so far as to imagine a bit of making out in some secluded corner.

"All the people handing out handfuls of swag to every little snot-nosed kid for a square mile gets uptight and offended if someone over the age of twelve tries to get in on the act. No, this will be better."

An hour later found them skulking in the shadows, waiting for stragglers to go by who weren't chaperoned by their parents. A group of three, aged maybe seven to nine, came down the root-buckled sidewalk with their bags already half filled with loot.

Cash jumped out of the darkness in front of them, mask in place and a baseball bat in one hand. With the other hand, he gestured for Sam to get behind them and block their escape. The kids shrieked, one boy dropping to the ground with his legs stuck out straight like one of those fainting goats that were all over the Internet. The other two, Batman and the chick from Frozen, clutched each other.

"Shut up," Cash barked at them, and the chunky pirate on the ground covered his head with his arms. "Just a bit of tribute, kiddies. Give me a handful of candy each, and you can head on out to replenish."

Sam stood holding the old rusted butcher knife Cash had given her to carry, her hood pulled low to obscure her face. She watched while the kids submitted to Cash rifling through their goody bags, shaking her head slightly when the pirate started to sob. Cash dropped the stolen sweets into a canvas bag tied to his belt, then stepped aside with a flourish.

"That's it, you can go," he said gruffly,

and laughed when they scampered down the sidewalk to the next streetlight. He headed back into the deeper dark beneath a maple tree, and waited for Sam to join him. "This is awesome—we pull the trick, *and* get the treat."

Sam leaned against the trunk beside him. "Those kids are going to tell an adult they got robbed. You know it's only a matter of time before some pissed-off parent comes looking for us."

Cash thought about that for a minute, then nodded. "Okay. Let's move over to Greenwood Avenue. There's a great hedge in the Mackley's front yard where we can hide."

Sam rolled her eyes, but followed him to the next street over. What was it she had seen in him again? Oh yeah, right; he was a loner slash bad boy who made up for lack of friends with a hokey put-on mystique. Mostly, she'd been drawn to his striking blue eyes. She glanced sideways at him, only able to make out the flat profile of the hockey mask in the darkness. She'd already come this far, she might as well keep on. Maybe the night would improve.

Cash robbed several more small groups of trick-or-treaters with Sam's reluctant back-up, moving from street to street through the neighborhood after each heist to avoid getting caught. It was after eleven when he finally checked his bag of booty and proclaimed, "Guess we should call it a night, huh? Got enough candy here to give diabetes to a hippo."

"Great," Sam said, smiling. "There's a marathon of horror flicks on the tube until six in the morning, so we can still catch a movie."

A small figure approached from down the street, and Cash ducked low, shushing Sam. The lone trick-or-treater, small enough to only be five or six years old, walked along the sidewalk fearlessly. He was dressed in a skeleton costume with a thin black cape trailing behind him, and a large plastic bag filled with goodies dragged at one arm.

Without warning, Cash jumped out onto the pavement, brandishing his baseball bat in one hand. "Hey there, little spook. Time to pay the toll."

"Come on, let's just call it a night," Sam

said, crossing her arms and frowning. Her hood was still pulled up, but the nearest lights revealed her un-masked face.

"Last one," Cash promised, looking down at the little boy. "Gimme a handful of candy, and you can pass."

The painted white face looked from Cash to Sam, and the kid dropped the heavy bag on the ground.

"One handful and you can go. Or I'll take it all," Cash threatened.

"Wow. I'm terrified," the boy said, and smiled. "This is the guy you've been gushing about?"

Sam rubbed her face tiredly. "He is kinda cute, even if he isn't very bright."

"Curfew's at midnight. You better finish, before Dad comes looking for us."

Cash's bright blue eyes went back and forth between them, and confusion was evident in his voice when he said, "You know this little brat?"

"Yeah, this is my brother, Damon," she said to Cash, then to the boy, "I've been trying to get him back to the house all night."

"Well, since you're Sam's brother,

guess you can keep your treats," Cash said, attempting to sound magnanimous.

"If you want, you can just do it now. It'll fit in here."

"Fine," she snapped. Another Halloween wasted.

"What'll fit in there?" Cash asked, leaning over to look when Damon opened the treat bag. There were suckers, SweetTarts, and fun size candy bars piled around something round and red. Damon jostled the bag a little, and the ball sized object shifted. There were two open eyes and a gaping mouth above the ragged remains of a bleeding neck.

Sam swung the butcher knife she'd carried all night. It was rusted and dirty, but still sharp enough to do the trick. The first chop cut through the back of his neck and the spinal cord. She grabbed a handful of greasy dark hair and swung once more. This time, the head came free. Sam dropped the knife beside the sprawled body of the boy she'd hoped to let reach second base.

"We're gonna be late," Damon pointed out, and Sam made a face at him. Then she dropped the bleeding head into the bag with the one her brother had already harvested, and picked it up by the plastic handles.

"I can't believe Halloween is already over," she said, stepping over the body. "Seriously, next year, I'm getting a better date."

Rose Blackthorn lives in the high mountain desert with her boyfriend and two dogs, Boo and Shadow. She spends her free time writing, reading, being crafty, and photographing the surrounding wilderness.

She is a member of the HWA and has appeared in *Stupefying Stories, Buzzy Mag, Interstellar Fiction, Jamais Vu,* and the anthologies *The Ghost IS the Machine, Enter at Your Own Risk: The End is the Beginning, FEAR: Of the Dark, Equilibrium Overturned,* and *Wrapped in Black: Thirteen Tales of Witches and the Occult,* among others.

More information can be found at roseblackthorn.wordpress.com.

WITCHES AND THE MARCH OF DIMES, AND MIKE WARNKE

by Babs Boden

In October of 1975, the year before we joined the charismatic church, I was a witch for Halloween. I was four and enamored with all things witchy. I wanted to grow up to look like Samantha Stevens, act like Endora, have socks like Witchie Poo, and possess the ability to morph in to an evil dragon like Maleficent. And also be married to either Keith Partridge or Johnny Gage, but only if they were down with witches.

When asked what I wanted to be for Halloween, I shouted "A witch!"

And a witch I was.

I had a pointy black hat, a flowing black dress, a long, scraggly black wig, and a broom. My face was painted with Kmart Halloween greasepaint—green, black, and gray—and one tooth was blacked out with black wax. My mother stood me in front of the full-length mirror in my bedroom to take it all in, and I promptly lost my shit.

"No, no, no! It's scary! Take it off! Take it off!" I cried, running in circles to get away from myself.

My very irritated mother wiped the paint off my face, and I did my trick-or-treating in my hat, dress, wig, and my own normal, boring, pasty face.

This was the same year that my sister's husband took me to the local March of Dimes haunted house. It was advertised heavily on TV, and I had been clamoring to go. Standing in line at the ticket booth, four-year-old me stood up on my tiptoes to stick my stupid moon face up to an opening cut in the side of the booth, and a large hairy hand reached out and grabbed my face. I think I wet my pants.

We filed past the operating-room scene, where a doctor with a Groucho Marx nose and glasses sawed in to a screaming, gore-soaked patient, pausing to inquire, "Would you like an aspirin?"

We walked past Dracula's coffin, where a Van Helsing-type brandishing a wooden stake and a mallet struggled to keep the Count in his coffin, while the ghoul looked *right at me* and hissed. I think I my pants again.

There were howling werewolves and slamming doors, and a dark black-lit maze where *things* brushed up against us.

Finally, in the basement lab of Dr. Frankenstein, I was on the verge of a hysterical little-kid nervous breakdown, so my brother-in-law asked The Monster to direct him to the nearest exit, pointing at me and telling him that I was terrified. The guy pulled off his mask, and gave us directions.

On the way home, I hid in the footwell in the backseat of my sister's Datsun, convinced that the surgeon, Dracula, the werewolf, and the owner of the hairy hand from the ticket booth were chasing us down the road.

Subsequent Halloweens sucked, as any kid who grew up in a churchy household well knows. Instead of dressing up like your favorite TV character or monster and roaming the neighborhood in the dark, acquiring pounds and pounds of delicious candy, you attended the church youth group "Harvest Festival" dressed as a either a hobo or your favorite Bible character. We sat on hay bales drinking apple cider, eating ginger snaps, and listening to recorded Mike Warnke sermons. Mike Warnke was an evangelist who claimed to have been a Satanist, and talked at great length about Halloween being a high holiday in the Satanist church, where they skin baby bunnies and drink blood and get up to all kinds of sex-and-drug-fueled Satan-y hijinks. He's the main reason that holy-roller kids like me got gypped out of Halloween for most of our childhoods...

As God is my witness, if I ever meet up with this guy (who has since been exposed as a massive fraud, of course) I will punch him dead in the face.

"That's for all the Milky Ways and Tootsie Rolls and Nestle Crunches and Hundred Thousand Dollar Bars you cost me, you son of a BITCH!"

Howdy Doody Time

by Kriscinda Lee Everitt

Laura sat in the living room, half-heartedly watching the live Halloween episode of *Ghost Hunters*, like she did every year while handing out candy. Her husband, Sam, was upstairs sleeping—in bed early to get up early in the morning to dig a grave.

He was the new cemetery caretaker. They had moved into their new home—on the cemetery grounds—toward the end of September. The small two-story sat just a moment's walk from the gates—a limestone affair whose front featured what looked like a wide, squat turret with a conical top. This resulted in a round living room and upstairs bedroom that proved difficult to furnish. It was perfect for Halloween. Perfect, except that, apparently, it was bad form to decorate for Halloween inside a cemetery. Thanksgiving would be fine. They could go all out for Christmas. But not Halloween.

It's a cemetery, for shit's sake.

She'd insisted on a pumpkin—to which

Sam had capitulated—but she wasn't allowed to carve it until the night before. And it had to be gone November 1. He'd even given her reason to believe that maybe he'd leave the gates open on Halloween night—at least for a little while, so that maybe some of the neighborhood kids could come in and trick-or-treat. So, she'd bought candy, carved her pumpkin, put a candle inside, and waited.

"They won't come in there, Laura," Sam would say. "It's a cemetery..."

"...for shit's sake," she'd finish.

"They won't even know to come in here," he'd say, zippering up his Carhartt jacket.

"I can put up a sign," she'd answer. "A few signs, so they know to come around the front. You said I could have one pumpkin. They can use it, as a beacon."

"Candy beacon."

"Yes." She'd smiled.

"I'll think about it. But don't get your hopes up. You might end up having to eat all that candy yourself."

"Oh no."

After they'd moved in, enjoying a lovely Indian summer, she'd taken to walking every day, as the cemetery was large—178 acres—and it contained several distinct areas, which she was learning to discern by their shapes and styles. There was a Jewish section, and a Chinese section. A children's section, and a section for the hundreds who'd died of a certain epidemic. There was a rich section, full of marble mausoleums, and a clerical section for Catholic priests and nuns (in separate micro-sections). A cemetery of the 19th-century Lawn Park style, it was beautiful, sprawling, and meticulously proper.

The grounds were full of Pin Oaks and Sugar Maples, Sourwoods and Sweetgums, all yellows, oranges, reds, and browns. The earthy russet scent made the air thick, and breathing it transported Laura back to the quieter, simpler times of her 1970s childhood where the eye- and mouth-holes of her stiff-plastic character masks pressed into her flesh, and the garbage bag-quality costume crinkled over her corduroy pants and velour shirt. She trick-or-treated with a pillowcase.

From the front porch, one could not see the gates of the cemetery, as the side of the house faced them. All up and down the opposite side of the street were houses, full of families, full of kids who'd been walking door to door, playing maybe a few tricks, but, by and large, gathering treats.

But now, it was dark. Laura could hear kids on the other side of the gate laughing, screeching with delight. The big bowl full of candy in the foyer sat sad and untouched. On the television, Josh Gates pulled a bad pun, which was completely ignored by the sound people as the overly dramatic spooky music lead everyone into a commercial.

This live broadcast needs a laugh track, Laura thought, just as a faint knock came to the front door.

She sat there for a moment, thinking she'd imagined it. A peel of children's laughter came from outside and she swore it seemed closer than the street.

They came in! Sam left the gates open! They must have seen the pumpkin!

Laura sprang from the couch, losing a slipper as she did. She flung the other off into the foyer, straightened out her candy corn motif sweater, grabbed the bowl, and took a deep breath, smiling wide, before she opened the door.

Here were her first trick-or-treaters for the night—at her new home—a little late, but here they were all the same.

"Trick or treat!" they sang in what should have been unison, but wasn't—the way only kids can do.

"Oh my!" She pretended to be frightened. These were not the costumes she'd expected. Most of them were handmade, but then, she'd read in *Real Simple*'s October issue that handmade was coming back, much to the horror of middleclass mothers everywhere. They must have been embracing it, because here they were—witches, sheet ghosts, a black cat, a devil. There were even a few of those plastic character masks of her own childhood, which must also have been coming back into vogue—Underdog, Wonder Woman, C-3PO. There was only one Teenage Mutant Ninja Turtle.

Laura grabbed handfuls of candy and threw them into buckets, bags, and baskets. And for the next hour, they came, with a soft knock, a "trick or treat," and they'd leave, giggling and laden with candy, until finally, the last.

He was a lone little boy, wearing a checked shirt and a bandana, but no hat. He had freckles painted on his face and his lips were big and bright red. He opened up his pillowcase—like she would have carried.

"Trick or treat, Mrs. Stanton!" he yelled with glee.

She leaned down to him.

"And who are you?"

"My name's Walter," he said, a little confused.

"No, no, I mean, who *are* you?" Laura laughed.

"Oh!" he said, figuring it out. "Why, I'm Howdy Doody!"

And he was. *Howdy Doody*. That was even before her time. That was her own *mother's* time. She couldn't believe this stuff was so popular now. She guessed this was what happened when homemade costumes came back into style—the grandparents made them because the parents were presumably too busy.

She threw a handful of candy into

Walter's bag, smiling. He cinched it shut and ran off the porch.

"Thank you, Mrs. Stanton!"

And he was gone.

Laura watched a little more *Ghost Hunters*, started to nod off on the couch, and then decided to go to bed.

As she crawled under the covers, Sam stirred. He reached a hand over, squeezed her arm, then let his arm fall limp again.

"Thank you," she said.

"Ferwuh?" he slurred, still half asleep.

"For keeping the gates open."

"Didn't," Sam said, then drifted back into slumberland.

Laura assumed he didn't really hear her, and soon fell asleep herself.

The morning of November 1 was bright and unseasonably warm, so after her usual cup of coffee, she thought she'd take her daily walk.

On the porch, she discovered her pumpkin missing—perhaps a Halloween causality of some local teens. The gates *were* open all night. She shrugged and hoped she wouldn't find it smashed over a statuette's head somewhere in the cemetery, or there'd definitely be no trick-or-treats next year.

She walked, inhaling the musty fall air, feeling wonderful and picking up the occasional stray candy wrapper. Some must have blown in from the street, except that the further into the cemetery she went, the more abundant they became, until she stopped dead on the paved road and looked straight ahead of her...into the children's section.

Here, there were candy wrappers everywhere, all over the graves. Snickers, Kit Kats, Milky Ways, Skittles, Jolly Ranchers, Whoppers—all of the candy she'd passed out the night before.

Laura stepped ahead into the section and walked slowly up and down the rows— wrappers *everywhere*. And then, when she stepped into the third row, there was her pumpkin. It sat unharmed, smiling up at her, from the grave of a Walter Beaumont, who died in 1957 at age ten.

Howdy Doody!

She stood there for a few minutes, processing, and then grabbed the pumpkin and took it back to the porch, hiding it out of the sight of visitors. She then returned to the children's section with a garbage bag and painstakingly picked up every wrapper. All this time, she processed, looking over her shoulder to make sure Sam wasn't around.

And she concluded two things—first, that next year, she'd make sure there was a wastebasket out here, and second, that she would have to figure something out for Christmas.

Kriscinda Lee Everitt is a writer and editor. Her stories have appeared in anthologies by **Permuted Press**, **Postscripts to Darkness**, and **Evil Girlfriend Media**. She is the founder/editor of *Despumation*, a journal publishing stories inspired by/based on extreme heavy metal music. She lives in Pittsburgh with her husband and two murderous cats.

WHEN I SCARED MYSELF OUT OF HALLOWEEN

by Jeremy Wagner

When I was a kid growing up in the 70s, Halloween was (and still is) my favorite holiday of the year. I've always been fascinated by things macabre, spooky, and scary. Well, except that one time, when I scared myself out of Halloween.

I loved trick-or-treating as a kid and was really into dressing up, from famous monsters to C-3PO. I think I started trick-or-treating around three years old, with my mom always buying me costumes I thought looked cool. At age four, I was really into witches, and begged my mom to buy me a witch costume and do my makeup. I'm sure I must've raised a few eyebrows, as a witch was probably looked at as being a "female role" that should be played out by little girls. Anyway, Mom did as I wished and got my costume on me and did my makeup. I'm surprised I didn't form a glam-metal band later in life.

Anyway, I digress here...it was when I was five that I decided I'd pick out my own costume, pick out the accessories, *and* do all the labor to dress myself—like a big boy. It was 1975, and I decided I wanted to be a vampire. My mom bought me a little vampire suit and cape—from either a JCPenney or Coast-to-Coast store. From there, I picked out some fangs and some horror makeup to go around my eyes. On Halloween night, before my mom took me out trick-or-treating to nearby farmhouses and country towns in central Wisconsin, I dressed myself, put the fangs in, and practiced my best Bela Lugosi accent.

"I vant to suck your bluuuuuuud."

Despite my determined and successful work at getting my costume on and my fangs in, I couldn't manage my makeup or hair. Mom wanted to give me a real vampiric face, so she slicked my hair back and sprayed it down to look like Dracula. I didn't care about quality-checking my mug in a mirror as I trusted she would do an amazing job.

As my mom did my makeup and hair, I

sat impatiently in a kitchen chair, fantasizing about how much candy I would get (and how much I could steal from my sister after we returned home from our Halloween rounds). Once my mom finished, she told me I looked awesome, and it was almost time to leave to trick-or-treat across the countryside.

This next part is the part I don't remember at all. From what Mom tells me, I had to go to go "pee-pee" before we left, so I raced up to the bathroom on the second floor of our farmhouse. Evidently, I relieved myself and, like a good boy, I went to wash my hands afterward. Now, as an adult, I'm around five foot three, so at age five, I was around three feet (haha) and always needed to use a small stool under the sink to wash my hands. I guess I pulled out the stool, stood on it, and prepared to wash my hands—and to my horror, found a monster staring back at me through the mirror above the sink. A mini-nightmare, a little ghoul with fangs, a corpse-white face, and dead black orbits hosting wide eyes...extremely wide eyes.

I froze up, I suppose, and somehow found the strength to pull myself away from the monster before me. Again, I don't remember this at all. I can't recall what I saw then, or how I got off the stool, and then hid in a corner of the bathroom. That's where Mom found me—curled up in a ball, unable to speak, frozen with terror in a corner of the bathroom.

What I saw above the sink was only my reflection (duh!), which I'd seen countless times before. But somehow my juvenile brain couldn't compute that the blood-sucking horror in the mirror was only a reflection of the badass FX job my mom did on my face.

Mom says she had to coax me gently out of the bathroom, assuring me that no monster was in there, that it was only my reflection I'd seen. That said, I guess Mom's reassuring words weren't good enough for me. I was so scared that I refused to go trick-or-treating, for fear that the vampire I saw was "out there somewhere." Worse, I wouldn't let my mom leave me alone all night, and I think I ruined that Halloween for my little sister, too. Sorry, Sis!

Hearing my mom tell me this story over the years made me learn a few things, like, I overcame that fear and dove back into Halloween and trick-or-treating by October 31, 1976. Moreover, I came to adore Halloween—and horror, for that matter— more and more, with extreme passion, through the rest of my childhood and into adulthood.

Sometimes you have to get scared shitless to realize you love it. Happy Halloween forever!

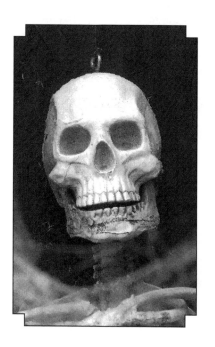

BEFORE THIS NIGHT IS DONE

by Barry Lee Dejasu

After passing a couple of unfamiliar houses, Shaina silently cursed, suspecting she'd taken a wrong exit into one of the neighboring towns. However, as she and her sister, May, drove past a familiar three-story Victorian, her doubts were put to rest. Shaina turned onto the next street as memories of the town of Baker came back to her.

"I think it's been almost eight years since I've been here." She scanned the area in the waning light, driving past a two-story brick building, its sign—U.S. POST OFFICE— worn and tired.

"I've *never* been here," May said.

"Sure you have. I mean, the last time we went trick-or-treating here, I was twelve and you were five..." Shaina trailed off as she glanced at the vampire queen in the passenger seat. She'd been away for only a few months, and was startled to discover that May had grown to be even less of the little girl she'd last seen. It was also a little disquieting to see her sister wearing such a racy outfit, but Mom hadn't seemed to mind. *I'll never get used to this*, she thought, and turned her attention back to the road.

"Mom always takes me to Rehoboth or Taunton," May said. "She says Baker is wicked sketchy."

Shaina snickered. "*Baker?* Sketchy? Please. She's just lazy—and *you've* been missing out on a treat."

"I don't know. We just never come out here."

"Well, *this* year you're lucky. We're gonna trick-or-treat here, together." Shaina turned onto Bridge Avenue, found a parking spot, and pulled over.

"Good," May said as Shaina turned off the car. "I want to get *lots* of candy before this night is done!"

Shaina snickered. "'Before this night is done?' Where'd you learn to talk like that?"

"Just because you're in *college* doesn't mean you're the only smart one," May said with an edge that only a newly-teenaged kid could produce.

Shaina smiled. "Touché."

They got out and looked around.

"I think..." Shaina scanned the block, recognized the wide windows and blocky stone stairs of the second house down. "There it is." She pointed. "They re-painted it. There used to be a big family who lived there that was *crazy*-generous with candy. Hopefully they're still there." She turned to May with a grin, which May returned emphatically.

They walked along the old asphalt and up a short flight of creaky wooden stairs. Shaina knocked on the gray door and turned to May, who grinned before shoving a set of vampire fangs into her mouth. In that moment, beneath the makeup and the costume, Shaina once again saw her kid sister, and she felt the surreal weight of *age* pressing down on her.

A full minute went by, so Shaina knocked again. They waited...and waited, but there was still no answer.

Her voice muffled by the fangs, May said, "They're not home."

"Guess not. Let's try someone else."

They headed back down to the street, but May hung back as Shaina passed the car. "We're not gonna drive?"

"Nah. The good thing about Baker is all the houses are in a giant zigzag. We can just go to the houses on each block, then it becomes the business district, and the road just loops around by the woods and brings us right back."

They continued on to the next street. There were a couple of houses with lights on, so they went to the first one. As they approached, Shaina saw a hand lowering one of the shades. *Oh, good*, she thought.

She led May to the door and knocked, and waited...

"What's up with that?" May asked.

"Hello?" Shaina called, trying to stay patient. She knocked again, but there was no answer. She put her ear to the door, prepared to step back in case it were to swing open; but nobody called out to her. Indeed, there was no other sound, not even of approaching footsteps from inside.

Shaina cursed, but managed to warp

the four-letter word into a guttural sound. "*Someone's* still got know something about trick-or-treating in this town."

"I don't think so," May said, and Shaina turned to her.

"What do you mean?"

"Trick-or-treaters." May turned and nodded at the silent street behind them. "There's no one else trick-or-treating out here."

Indeed, they didn't see or even hear a single other person as they moved up to the next block. Shaina then noticed the lack of decorations: no jack-o'-lanterns on porches or doorsteps, no fake cobwebs or electric candles in any of the windows, no white cloth ghosts or even ribbons of toilet paper hanging in trees.

Shaina didn't want to give up just yet, and they tried a few more houses; however, there were almost no signs of life at any of them. At one point, Shaina made clear eye contact with a wide-eyed woman peeking through a window, but the woman quickly turned away, and didn't answer the door when they knocked.

After the sixth unwelcoming house in a row (now on the second stretch of houses in the zig-zag), Shaina turned away from her perplexed sister and let her breath out through pursed lips.

A jet flew by overhead, and as its warbling roar vanished, Shaina noticed the palpable silence around them: no birds or bats chirped, no dogs barked, no insects buzzed. She realized she'd not even seen a single car since they'd entered Baker; it was like the whole town was hiding. As the streetlights began to flicker on, she shivered.

They were standing across from the "business district," which was little more than a cluster of squat buildings that sported a bank branch, a Laundromat, and a couple of stores. She briefly recalled evenings with an old boyfriend here, running through the interconnected alleys between two of the buildings to get to his home. Like their relationship, time hadn't helped the business district; the stores were pockmarked by empty spaces, their doors sealed tight, windows papered over in reluctant goodbyes.

"What the *fuck?*" May said. Shaina

practically jumped out of her skin at the unexpected F-bomb.

She glared at May, who shrugged. *Seriously though*, Shaina thought. "I'm so sorry, May. This is totally ruining the evening."

"It's okay," May said. "It's not ruined. We can just go back home and trick-or-treat there."

"I've just never seen anything like this."

Dusk had started to light up the stars above, although the local weather station's promised clouds were beginning to creep in from the horizon. It wasn't supposed to rain until long after midnight, but Shaina still wanted to get back to the car before she needed to break out the flashlight on her keychain. She glanced at her watch. "It's still early. Let's go."

Shaina watched May's face as they walked down the street. May was annoyed and disappointed, but luckily that seemed to be all. She wasn't a little kid anymore; that was for sure. She'd come a long way from her days of crying and throwing tantrums, but then, she'd always been good about—

Shaina stopped, listening. Her and May's shadows were stretched out in the murky yellow pool of light from the streetlamp behind them.

May said, "You heard it, too?"

"Yeah. Sounded like a door shutting or something."

They waited for some kind of follow-up to the sound; some kind of an address from one of the residents, maybe even an apology for their tardy courtesy, but there was only more of that uncomfortable silence.

Shaina shrugged, hiking her jacket up around her frame. "Well, let's go..."

The sound came again, louder. *Not a door*, Shaina thought distantly as she searched for the source. It had come from the farthest house to their right, in the wooded area beside it. The crackling thump reminded her of deer in the forest, all but invisible until their heavy feet fell on the brush beneath.

"What *was* that?" May asked, her voice low.

"Let's...just get back to the car," Shaina said.

Another thump, louder. Not just

louder—it came from another direction. Shaina tried to place the sound, saw only the concealing forms of the half-lit houses around them, felt the cold, phantom hands of fear glide down on the space between her shoulders, and the sensation spread quickly through her chest.

"Shaina?"

"May, just...come closer."

May came over and grabbed Shaina's hand; the jack-o'-lantern's plastic handle was hard and intrusive in her grip, but there was something comfortingly familiar and *normal* about it.

Another crunching thump came, and there was no denial of its approaching proximity this time. May moved closer beside Shaina. Another impact, behind them now, and Shaina once again found herself thinking of footsteps.

"What is that?"

"I—" Shaina shook her head, eyes wide, as a new crash boomed from just behind one of the houses. "I don't know. Let's...just stay under the lights and go back this way."

There was a moment of silence as they

made their way down to the intersection and crossed the street to the business district. As they neared the bank, they heard it again: *Crunch!* May's hand clamped down hard on Shaina's, and they both stopped.

Crunch!

"Shay..." May's breath ran out on the syllable, and Shaina saw her wide eyes focused on something in the distance. She turned—

The shape beside the house could've been anything; it was too short and shapeless to appear outwardly threatening. It was a blurry silhouette against the dim ambience of the streetlight across the way, indistinct in form; but when it ducked out of sight around the corner of the house, Shaina felt her breath die in her lungs. A moment later, she noticed a light in one of the windows only after it winked out, hidden or smothered.

"Jesus," Shaina hissed as she half-pulled, half-pushed May into the glass annex at the front of the bank. They pressed themselves to the glass, and Shaina heard May's breath coming and going in quick hisses.

"Just calm down," Shaina said. "I mean...we don't even know what's going on."

She fleetingly recalled a group of pranksters in Providence who shot films of themselves dressed up as a giant, creepy snowman and jumped at passers-by, scaring the living daylights out of them in the name of Internet humor. "For all we know, this is just a—"

"Shaina..."

May's tone injected a shiver into the base of Shaina's neck that rattled her whole body. She turned to find May pointing at the two cars parked directly across the street—and the unsteady movements of the dark shape crouching behind them, peering above the bumper and hood. For a long moment, they just stared at it. It was too round, too wide, to be a person. Fueled by some kind of desperate hope, Shaina craned her neck to get a better look, but as soon as she did, the shape dropped down out of sight. She didn't breathe—she just stared, and waited.

Just as suddenly as it had vanished, it reappeared around the back of the farthest car, something huge, as tall as the vehicle beside it, and nearly as long. It squatted closely to the ground, too dark to see clearly, but its gray hue distinct enough from the dusk around it.

Shaina heard May's voice keening in the back of her throat, but she couldn't take her eyes off the thing, not even as it began to rise up. Then it jumped—no, it *stretched* its upper half straight toward them, getting impossibly long—

Then they were running.

It was a wild, screaming run, directionless save for getting *away*. Halfway down the block, Shaina remembered a way between the buildings, and steered May into the alley, a plan beginning to form. As their shoes crunched on the gravelly asphalt, Shaina urged May to keep going until they emerged in the shadowy back alley. They stopped to catch their bearings, as well as their breaths.

"Shaina?" May said, her voice quivering with tension. "Where are we *going?*"

"Back...to the car," Shaina gasped. She led them into a connecting alley to the right. A wooden platform had been added to the alley's upper half in the years since she'd last been here; it looked like some kind of storage area. The resulting tunnel beneath the wood was perfectly dark, save for the promising glow of an exit at the other end, in the middle of the black.

"But we didn't come this way..."

"We'll cut through to the other side of these buildings, and then we'll be only a block and a half from the car." She found herself unable to calculate the actual distance, but she wouldn't start questioning herself now.

May shoved her hand into Shaina's and said, "Let's go."

It was dark and cold in the tunnel, and their awkward footsteps were the thunderous in the low-ceilinged darkness. The tunnel smelled, too—it smelled *bad*; rancid, rotting, and cloying, Shaina had to literally pinch her nostrils with her free hand to shut the stench out.

There was a scraping sound, and Shaina's heart leapt into her throat, but May apologized, murmuring something about the ground. Shaina turned to her, but saw only more of that horrible blackness that threatened to drown her senses. Turning back to the expanding rectangle of light and open air ahead, she was grateful that May couldn't see her own look of fear.

117

"It smells *so* gross in here," May said. Shaina was actually somewhat relieved that May was paying more attention to the smell than the darkness around them.

God, could Shaina have forgotten how *long* the alley was? It had been years since she'd been down here, sure, and the wood above them had never been there; plus, she'd also never been through it at night. Even so, it was like the tunnel was getting longer before them.

"Why are we slowing down?" May asked.

"It's an optical illusion," Shaina said, almost more to herself. "We're just disoriented." They were getting closer to the other end, for sure; it was just hard to tell in the absolute black of the tunnel. "Just go straight and hold my hand. You're doing fine."

They kept walking. Soon the tunnel began to widen and brighten as they neared the end. Shaina looked down and could see her own feet beneath her. She let a half-forgotten breath out of her protesting lungs.

They emerged into the dim light of a loading area behind one of the business district's buildings. There was the back of the liquor store, the old Subway, so the other alley had to be...

"Which way?" May asked, but Shaina's narrowed eyes slowly widened as a sick, sinking feeling formed in her stomach.

There were only walls facing them. No alley, no passage...just this cul-de-sac.

Shaina blinked, looked around rapidly. No. *No.* This wasn't it. This wasn't how it had always been. Could they have even just entered the *wrong* alley? No, she'd remembered correctly—this was it. *But then...*

"Shaina?" May asked.

"Oh *shit*," Shaina heard herself say, but she didn't care about that right now.

"What?"

"This is some kind of loading dock, but it's all closed off." She took a deep breath, let it out in a heavy, shaking sigh and pointed at the bright, new-looking bricks, maybe only a year old. "That wall...it didn't used to be there."

"So we're *trapped?*" Shaina could hear the panic rising in May's voice. She hoped there was *something* she could say to comfort her sister, but she knew that this was pathetic optimism. Pursing her lips, she turned and nodded at the black eye of the tunnel.

"No...but we have to go back through *there* again."

They gave each other a long look. Shaina pulled out her keys and turned the flashlight on. It was one of those tiny things that you had to squeeze to keep the tiny LED shining, but it produced a mercifully bright halo of amber-colored light. She trained the beam on the ground before them, and felt May take her hand. Holding her breath, Shaina led them back into the dark.

The smell didn't seem as bad this time; perhaps they'd gotten used to it, or perhaps they were moving in the same direction as the air currents. It still stank like the lowest circle of hell, however, and Shaina kept her face scrunched as they walked.

The alley once again had that disorienting illusion of growing longer, narrower, but Shaina pushed on, trying to think of where they would go next. They would return to the front of the business district and, keeping an eye out for...that *thing*, they would go directly to the nearest house and—

And what? Wait there? Hide out like everyone else? Call animal control?

A wet scraping sound came from nearby, but May didn't claim responsibility this time. Shaina began to walk a little faster, squeezing May's hand.

"Shaina, was—?"

"Don't pay attention to it," she said. "Just keep walking. We're almost there."

Something cold and smooth brushed against the side of Shaina's face. She screamed, and there was absolute darkness as her fingers released the flashlight's button. Shaina cranked her head to the side as the skin-crawling feeling of *damp* began to register along her violated jaw and cheek. Shaina felt May's hand slip out of her own, and May screamed.

"I'm right here, May!" Shaina said, reaching up and feeling her cold keys jab her cheek painfully; thinking better of it, she wiped at her face with the sleeve of her jacket. "Just calm dow—*fuck!*"

The end of the tunnel seemed to have

gotten farther away again.

"Shaina?"

"Sorry, there was a—"

She felt something soft brush against her free hand's fingers, and she snatched her arm back a split second before realizing it was May's own cold hand seeking comfort; she took it and pulled her closer. Fumbling for the flashlight on her keys again, Shaina said with surprising calm, "Come on, Sis, let's just get out of here."

"Shaina, wait! I can't see you."

"It's okay," Shaina said. "Just hold my hand and follow me."

"Okay, but where *are* you?"

Shaina stopped, feeling ice water pump into her veins. Turning back, she maneuvered the flashlight until it was focused on her sister, standing several feet away. One of May's hands had a white-knuckled grip on the handle of the jack-o'-lantern...and the other, Shaina saw, hung empty by her side.

Something black and glistening lowered itself from the ceiling directly behind May, just as the hand in Shaina's squeezed.

Darkness enveloped the tunnel once

again, and with it—screams.

Something rammed into Shaina, and she tore away from it, but the gibbering cries belonged to a terrified May. Grabbing her real and wonderfully *warm* hand, Shaina started running.

The tunnel stretched onward. The more they ran, the farther away the light at the end seemed to be. There were more sounds around them, which Shaina ignored as best as she could; the darkness seemed to snatch at her jacket and her feet, but she tore through the unseen brambles, her feet somehow moving faster beneath her.

Now, the light ahead was getting brighter, closer.

Wispy shadows smacked a sticky, unseen cobweb on her face. With a terrified, disgusted grunt, she tried to wipe it away but felt only the dry coarseness of her sleeve against her skin.

As the mouth of the tunnel reluctantly yawned around them, she kept running until they emerged into the dim but welcoming light of the adjoining alley once again, and Shaina had a moment of panic when she thought she'd dropped her keys; but May held them up, smiling weakly. They embraced each other with shivering sobs.

After a long moment, they crept back between the buildings near the street, stopping just short of the sidewalk. Leaning in, Shaina whispered, "If that thing is still out there, we need to go somewhere else."

"Where? How?"

Shaina bit her lip, looking around. She could see a streetlamp and a car nearby; on the other side of the street were the two cars that the thing had hidden behind. Keeping her eyes on it, she said, "C'mon."

They moved into the nightmarishly silent street again. Shaina fixed her gaze on the two cars across the way, and waited. There was no movement that she could see, and that was precisely what worried her.

She stared for a good, long time. Taking a deep breath, she waited...

"*Go!*"

They sprinted in the opposite direction up the street. They had made it nearly to the end of the block when a sound came from behind them, a muffled, crunching pursuit on the pavement.

They made a tight left around the general store—

Light.

A spot of light—beautiful, brilliantly bright *light* had appeared dead ahead. It moved, pointed directly at Shaina and May for a moment, then switched up once, twice, three times before pointing down, and just visible in the ambience above it—an insistently beckoning hand and the shine of eyeglasses.

Oh my fucking god! Shaina wasn't sure, but didn't particularly care, if she'd said it aloud. She and May tore along the block to the house, charged up the steps atop which the woman stood. Then a whole *doorway* of light was opened, and Shaina was vaguely aware of the harsh, urgent words the woman whispered as they entered the surreal familiarity of a warm, bright living room. They turned and watched as the woman jumped inside and slammed the door shut behind her.

"What are you two *doing?*" the woman hissed, turning to switch the bolt on the door and crossing the room towards them. She slammed the flashlight down on a wide, wooden table near the door before stomping, stony-faced, past them.

"We were—" Shaina blurted, trying and failing to find some sane way of describing their evening. "There's something out—"

The woman spun to them, her eyes narrow behind their wide lenses. Shaina abruptly recognized her, realized just where they'd wound up, but she said nothing as the woman shouted, "It's *after hours*! Are you two *crazy*?"

Some decorations and furniture were new or different, but it was all coming back to Shaina now; the coziness, the warmth, the smell of freshly-baked bread...

Shoving her keys in her pocket, Shaina led May into the living room, where their unexpected hostess had them sit down on a couple of big, comfy chairs—the very same ones that Shaina remembered.

The woman left them and went into the kitchen. After a time, Shaina said, "Mrs. Hull...do you remember me?"

Mrs. Hull stood in the kitchen doorway,

an oven mitt over her left hand and a puzzled look on her face.

"It's me, Shaina. I...I used to date Kevin?"

Mrs. Hull's eyes widened, and she stepped farther into the living room. "Oh my God...Shaina?"

"Yes, it's me! Oh Mrs. Hull, *what* is go—?"

"Oh, look at you! Wow, you're a young *woman* now, aren't you?"

Shaina took an uneven breath. "Yeah, I guess, but—"

"You really hurt him, you know."

"What?" Shaina frowned.

"He was okay *later*, of course," Mrs. Hull continued, shaking her head and closing her eyes. "But oh, that was a *long* year." She opened her eyes, looking away now, into some distant memory, and her face darkened. "Then he joined Bestwick Construction, and they uncovered all those tunnels out in the woods..." She shook her head, glaring at Shaina, who only then noticed the tears collecting along the rim of Mrs. Hull's eyes. "And then he and the other workers... *vanished*, and then—"

"Mrs. Hull," Shaina interrupted, and was rewarded with silence. "Please. I don't know *anything* about any of this. I've not been here in years, and—"

"I'm scared!" May said, her voice cracking slightly, and Shaina went silent. She and Mrs. Hull looked at May, whose eyes were wide, but no tears accompanied her heavy, uneven breaths. "Please, Mrs. Hull," May added, sounding younger than ever. "We just wanted to go trick-or-treating, but something *scary* is going on out there. Please help us!"

"I'm so sorry," Mrs. Hull said. "Wait, are you—?" She turned to Shaina. "Is this little Mallorie?"

"It's just May," May said.

"Oh wow, listen to her!" Mrs. Hull said, beaming like everything was normal. "Hold on, I just have to check on the bread." She waved her mitt at them, grinning. "I always bake during the curfew."

She disappeared back into the kitchen, and May and Shaina looked at each other. Shaina had so many questions swirling in her mind, so she took the moment to line them up in some semblance of order before she bombarded Mrs. Hull with them.

"There we go," Mrs. Hull said, as she re-emerged from the kitchen. "All set."

The lights went out.

All background noise was silenced. The room was still warm, but the interruption brought a heavy chill nonetheless.

"Oh no...*oh no*," Mrs. Hull muttered from somewhere nearby. "Just...wait. Don't move." She made a breathless snicker and, unable to deliver her intended humor, said, "Don't want to knock anything over, do we? Heh."

Shaina immediately thought of the tunnel, of how pitch-black it had been, how bad that *smell* had been. She wrinkled her nose, almost smelling that thick, cloying odor all over again—

Stop it, she commanded herself. *You're safe. You're fine now.*

"Mrs. Hull," Shaina said, licking her dry lips. "*What* is going on here?"

"A compromise," Mrs. Hull said. "Every residence has its compromise. We wait inside at night as they make their rounds, and—"

she broke off and made a sound like a gasp or a hiccup. After a long moment, she cleared her throat.

"Shaina," May said in a low voice.

"Sorry, Sis," Shaina said, patting furiously at her jacket for her keys. "Just trying to get my—"

Lights, background noise; everything came back on.

Shaina took a heavy breath and looked at May. Her sister's eyes were wide, glancing around with quick movements. When they finally fixed on Shaina, she smiled pathetically, and Shaina weakly returned it.

They turned to find Mrs. Hull walking over, pulling the mitt off her hand. "You probably want to get back to your car."

Shaina turned to the curtained windows.

"Oh, don't worry," Mrs. Hull said, smiling.

"Mrs. Hull, *what is going on?*" Shaina asked. She hooked her thumb at the window. "Those *things* out there were—"

"Don't be afraid," Mrs. Hull repeated, and dropped the mitt on the floor.

Shaina picked up the mitt and handed

it back to her. Mrs. Hull's hands rose, but she didn't take the proffered mitt. Instead she reached up and took her glasses off and dropped them to the floor.

Shaina felt her pulse quicken.

Mrs. Hull lifted her hands once again, holding them before her face like the most important step in the game of hide-and-seek, plating her fingertips at different points. She squeezed, pulled, and the face beneath split swiftly with the sound of a watermelon being opened.

Shaina lunged to her feet, grabbing May and dragging her toward the door. They slammed against it. Ambient shadows, squirming with ever-moving enthusiasm, manifested on the door before them, and the half-glimpsed visage became even more frightfully detailed in Shaina's mind.

Shaina groped at the door's bolt as the stench from the tunnel returned in full force, but now more pronounced, *riper*. Chuckling, wet chortles rose behind her, sounding like no laugh she'd ever heard.

Fortunately, the bolt was well-greased, and turned easily when Shaina twisted it.

She pulled it open and May shoved past her just as appendages—possibly still hands—brushed Shaina's jacket as she launched herself past the open door and into the night.

Shaina tripped over a raised crack of cement at the next corner, but kept herself upright and stole a look to make sure May was still running with her. They rounded the corner just as the horrible, bulky *crunch* hit the pavement behind them.

As they turned into the middle part of Baker's zig-zag, another of those horrible *things* spilled out from behind a house at the end of the block. It stopped at the end of the lawn, a hulking mass of twitching, glistening gray, seeming to watch them with unseen eyes as they ran by. Shaina shouted wildly and snatched at one of May's swinging hands, hauling her closer as they ran down the block and toward Bridge Avenue again.

The car was waiting for them, and they couldn't have arrived sooner, for two more of those things were arcing toward them on the ground with fluid loping movements, crunching on the pavement as they approached. Shaina opened the driver's door and shoved May in headfirst, and May wordlessly scrambled into the passenger seat. Jumping in after her, Shaina slammed the door shut just as one of the things moved in beside the car.

Shaina heard screaming, and her spasming hands somehow found her keys and stabbed one into the ignition—but it was the wrong one. The screams got louder, and Shaina realized *she* was making them. As she removed the key, something slammed against the driver's-side window, and she ducked back instinctively and dared to look.

The gray mass spread out on the window, rippling with horrible animation, and a *face* began to appear.

The keys!

Tearing her eyes away from the face, trying not to think about how only inches and safety glass separated her from it, Shaina fumbled with the keys, found the one with the green loop around it, jammed it into the ignition, and the car came to amazing life.

Shaina throttled the gearshift, hit the lights—

The face twisted against the windshield,

and Shaina recognized the features as it opened its mouth and *licked* at the filthy glass obscenely. Screaming, she hit the gas, and the face disappeared as the car shot forward.

• • •

Shaina didn't stop driving until she felt her adrenaline cloud begin to subside. How far had they gone? *Where* had they gone? It didn't matter.

There had been silence in the car for some time now, and Shaina finally looked over at May, who sat facing directly ahead, eyes wide and glassy, the corners of her mouth curled slightly down.

"How...how are you doing over there?"

May didn't blink as she croaked, "I'm fine."

Shaina slowly took her foot off the gas. They were approaching one of the hills just before their hometown, and the car began to slow. "May?"

May remained featureless as she muttered, "I'm fine."

"You've not said a word since..." Shaina

couldn't finish the sentence.

"Neither have you."

Shaina pulled the car over. Maybe three hundred feet up the road, her headlights were just starting to show the WELCOME sign for their hometown.

May turned and looked at her. Her eyes were wide, unmoving and unreadable. Shaina's heart broke for her; she bit her lip, looked away, felt her own eyes stinging. It was a horrible, heartbreaking way for May's childhood to end.

"I'm sorry," Shaina said. "I'm away all the time now. I barely get to see you anymore. I just wanted us to reconnect. I just wanted to have *fun* with you again, trick-or-treating." She shook her head, feeling tears form. "I'm so sorry."

May said something, and Shaina sniffed back her tears and self-pity. There would be plenty of time to cry later; right now, she had to be the big sister that May needed. She composed herself and asked, "What was that?"

May's hands rose and pressed to the sides of her face. "Trick-or-treat," she repeated, and tore off the mask.

Barry Lee Dejasu lives in Providence, Rhode Island. A contributing editor for Shock Totem, he's also an author, media journalist, moviegoer, music collector, and book hoarder.

THE MANSION

by Lee Thomas

In high school, the popular kids partied at a place called "The Mansion." Not being one of the popular kids I only heard about excursions to the mansion after they'd occurred, usually on Mondays while the Pops rushed to classes, talking about how wasted they'd gotten.

Though not unpopular, I was at best a non-entity to my classmates, another face in the crowd, another body around which to navigate as they moved from one class to the next. As such, I was surprised when one of the football players, let's call him "Mike," invited me to The Mansion for a Halloween kegger. He even offered me a ride.

The Mansion was exactly that. It was situated in a small, wealthy area called Medina not far from Bellevue, WA. The place took up a block, which had a single street light on the near corner, leaving the bulk of the extended cul-de-sac in shadows. The design of the house could be roughly described as Modern Mediterranean, with archways and white walls and a tiled roof. Outside, damage was visible but not extensive. A broken window. A lone bit of graffiti on one corner of the facade. I know it was there, but I can't remember what it depicted.

Inside, cosmetic and structural abuse flourished. The place had been gutted. One empty room with scarred and pitted walls followed another. Graffiti climbed like mold on the remaining surfaces. Beer cans lined the baseboards. In the center of the living room, a hole punched through to the basement. It was roughly eight feet in diameter. More than one drunk student had fallen through it over the course of the school year.

The electricity had been shut off long ago, so the only lights, mostly centered around the keg and cups in a back hallway, were camp lanterns and flashlights.

Mike disappeared about thirty seconds after we arrived, leaving me to wander the scene. Though I'm sure a few of my classmates had taken the time to don costumes, most of us milled through the shadows in our usual clothes: t-shirts, polo shirts, jeans, khakis. The setting was a more than adequate acknowledgement of the macabre holiday.

I came across a friend of mine, David, and his giggly girlfriend on the staircase. They made out in the soft glow of a boom box. UFO's "Love to Love" glided with bluesy grandeur from the small speakers. Conversation wasn't on their agenda so I moved on.

Though I said, "hello" to a lot of people, I was mostly on my own, too nervous around my peers to instigate a conversation, too uncertain of myself to flirt with any of the girls (and frankly, not particularly driven to do so). I'd always felt removed, disconnected from the majority of my peers. Easier to keep my head down and not chance conversation. This feeling was intensified by the laughter around me.

In the living room, I paused at the edge of the hole and looked down. No lights there, but movement. Shadows writhed within shadows. Darkness embraced itself and turned slowly so that no side went untouched. As I lost myself in the black motion, fear settled in, though I couldn't exactly pin my fear on any one thing. I knew my classmates moved below, but for a time, I imagined only space, deep and infinite. I also imagined what lived in that space, wondering on the kinds of plans it had for me.

Years later, I wrote a story about this experience. It's been trunked. I could never work out the kinks. Much of that night has stayed with me, though, despite the drinking. On that night I discovered that dread didn't need a face, a knife, teeth, or claws. Sometimes dread was simply *nothing* and staring at that nothing, fearing you will one day become a part of it.

ALLHALLOWTIDE
(TO THE FAITHLESS
DEPARTED)

by Sydney Leigh

My heart beats wildly inside my sinking chest,
          loud like a *BOMB* in my head

The clowns come too close,
laughing and running endless circles around me
  in
oversized shoes,
      slapping the floor in psychotic
                    rhythmic
              patterns

They breathe down my neck,
   hot air burning my skin

stingingmelikebees

      I want to *SCREAM*, but I can't—
             it's so dark and I can't see
             I can feel the spiders
             silently crawling down from

the murderous sky,
running over my feet and

f
a
l
l
i
n
g

into my hair
but I can't pull them out—
        someone is tying my hands behind my back
        I don't know who it is   his skin is
                cold and wet

        and I can smell the spoiled milk,
                hear it dripping onto the
rotted floor
        it's so . . .
                        sour
        it's biting the insides of my nose and
making my head ache,
the bomb is ticking away—
I prepare for the boom and it's

ALLHALLOWTIDE

Now
I hear the snakes,
their pitchfork tongues cursing as they slither,
coming from the water to take me back with
them

                              (I don't want to go—
the water is so cold)

                              and I can't see anything.
                              Who's talking to me?

I hear voices and they're calling out,
          offering love and religion and
          all I could never believe . . .
                    Pay no attention to the man
                    with the cold, wet hands because

                    salvation
                    salvation
                    s-a-l-i-v-a-t-i-o-n

                    Digest your faith with enzymes!
          Then come and have some candy, little girl . . .

Every time
you clear your throat,
a doorbell rings
in hell.

Sydney Leigh is the evil literary double of a mostly sane writer and editor who hails from the North Shore. She and her one-eyed muse sweep the misty mountainsides of Valhalla with falcons on their shoulders, searching for dark stories to tell...and they both have scars to prove it. You can find her short fiction and poetry in various anthologies and magazines, and more is due to appear in several forthcoming collections.

Look for her at **Villipede Publications**, where she spends her days charming letters and constructing nightmares—or drop into her website at www.shawnaleighbernard.com.

FLAY BELLS RING, OR HOW THE HORROR FILMMAKER STOLE CHRISTMAS

by Mike Lombardo

Halloween is a very special time of year for me. It's a season that brings out the creativity in people and it's the one time of year when I'm not thought to be criminally insane by the common populace. Well, most of the time, anyway...

It was October the first, in the year of our Lord two thousand and four. I was gleefully putting the final touches on what at the time was my finest Halloween set-up to date: A full Christmas massacre set piece that would encompass my entire driveway and front yard. Visitors would approach the house, beckoned forward by twin lines of light-up candy canes marking the path up the driveway, which itself was lined with delicately wrapped Christmas presents, many of which were leaking blood from the bottoms. Long strings of colorful Christmas lights adorned ropes of barbed wire, scraps of bloodied flesh intermittently dangling next to shiny ornaments. A decapitated corpse bound like a mummy in snowman wrapping paper and shiny gold ribbon sat against the garage door. The Christmas stocking still containing a leg hung neatly next to a blood-smeared sign proclaiming that visitors were in fact at Santa's Workshop. It was below this sign that I would sit, my Santa suit resembling a collaboration between Jackson Pollack and Jeffrey Dahmer.

It's worth mentioning that I live in a very conservative and religious suburban area that has all but eliminated Halloween from existence. The myriad of churches that cover the landscape like festering sores hold "Harvest Festivals" on trick-or-treat night to keep children indoors and to prevent them from wearing costumes of "devils, demons, and other ungodly things." Homes with Halloween decorations are a rare sight where

I live. So to say that my neighbors were displeased with my décor would be a bit of an understatement. The first indicator of their displeasure took the form of the nightly vandalism of my set piece. Every morning I would wake up before school and pick up the kicked over candy cane lights, reposition the blood-soaked presents, and put the Santa's Workshop sign back up. Every night I would turn on the Christmas lights, shout "Ho ho ho!" into the cold autumn air, and go to sleep. This daily ritual went on until trick-or-treat night.

The kaleidoscope of colored lights glinted off of my slimy purplish and mottled flesh as I sat in my chair beckoning trick-or-treaters to come up and tell me what they wanted for Christmas. I told the ones that refused to come closer that they had made my Naughty List and that I would be seeing them soon. I punctuated this threat with a menacing, blood-drooling smile and a wave. Surprisingly the parents of most of the kids got a huge kick out of everything and many even asked to take pictures of their children posing with me. I had some good conversations about the bizarre lack of Halloween spirit in Lancaster and many parents shared my sentiment that even just ten years ago, every house on the block would have converted their garage into a Chamber of Horrors and that they knew that Halloween was just harmless fun. Overall it was a very successful night.

Flash forward to early November. The corpse of Halloween was barely cold and already the radio airwaves were blasting an endless loop of "Little Drummer Boy" and that really annoying Paul McCartney Christmas song. I was slaving away at my day job in the pizza shop when an irate woman walks in the door. She looks at me for a moment, delivers a death stare, and then approaches the counter.

"What can I do for you, ma'am?" I ask politely.

"You ruined Christmas for my child!" she spat.

I stare at her puzzled for a moment, and then realize she is referring to my Halloween decorations. The question then becomes how the hell did she know who I was and where I worked? Before I could ask her, she launched into an angry tirade about how her daughter is now terrified of Santa Claus and that I destroyed Christmas for her family and I should be ashamed of myself. She went on to tell me that it's offensive to her as a Christian that I would twist Yuletide imagery into something so horrific. I politely informed her that Santa and his reindeer and the like were mainly derived from Germanic pagan tradition mixed with a healthy dose of Hallmark marketing blitzkriegs to sell scented candles and cheap greeting cards. She merely huffed and repeated that her child is traumatized now and I should be ashamed of myself. I ended the conversation by politely asking her why, if she was so concerned about her daughter's mental being, would she bring her to a house on Halloween night that was decorated with Christmas lights and dismembered body parts? She turned and left without another word and I never saw her again. I mulled over this for the rest of my shift and I finally came to the conclusion that if I was able to psychologically scar just one child on Halloween, then my job here was done.

Merry Christmas, everyone, and Happy Halloween!

THE CANDLE EATERS

by K. Allen Wood

Katie Adams cut a white swath through the dark of the woods, a ghost to all but the dead.

The crisp night air was its own special vintage, and it soothed her lungs as she weaved between the shadows. A soft breeze caressed her with the smells of October: smoldering brush piles; damp, hungry soil; the breath of cold brick chimneys just waking from their summer-long slumber.

It was her favorite time of the year. The in-between, when the bushes and trees strutted their autumn wardrobes and the wind endlessly whispered the promise of winter.

She emerged from the woods and into a field on the edge of Farmington Circle. The tall grass and weeds whipped across her thighs as she ran toward the small isolated community of Bridgetown Pines.

As she reached the sidewalk, she slowed and caught her breath. She plucked a few sticky burrs from the tattered sheets that made up her ghostly costume, and cast them away. Under the canopy of oaks that lined the street, Katie let the beauty of twilight calm her as only it could. Like a cleansing rain, the night descended and washed away her loneliness, the anger she harbored toward her mother, and the fear of what lay ahead now that her father was gone.

Grief and regret were such destructive things, parasitic emotions which feast upon sorrow and pain. Katie had learned this the hard way, having played host to the vile things for the past six months, worrying over what could have been done differently, words that could have been said more often. But she had found no answers in what *could* have been, only in what *is*. So she'd fought back, fought hard, and though her battle was yet won, though she still struggled with the pain and anger and despair, she had a stranglehold on her suffering.

And she wasn't letting go.

Her mother, on the other hand, had given up, had given in to the crippling heartache that weighed down upon them both. Katie felt like she'd shed more tears for the metaphoric loss of her mother than for the real, knife-to-the-heart passing of her father.

Tonight, though, this final October night, she would let it all go, for however brief a moment. Tonight she would once again embrace the wonders of childhood.

For some reason, however, as she continued down the street, her empty pillowcase swinging at her side, Katie had the strange feeling that something was amiss, as if the shadows held secrets best left in the dark. The neighborhood beyond was dead calm, as always; the lawns and shrubbery immaculately groomed and swaying gently in the breeze, but somehow...wrong. The knotted fingers of the trees seemed to loom a bit closer. The symphony of night-sounds—insects, birds, small animals rustling in the leaves—was hushed.

Goose bumps prickled her skin. She picked up her pace.

She tried to push her unease aside, ascribe it to overactive imagination, but the feeling dogged her all the way to 18

Farmington Circle, where it evaporated like morning mist.

Katie skipped up the driveway—perhaps a little faster than normal—and onto the cobblestone path leading to the side door. Twin wicker chairs sat empty on the wooden patio, a deck of cards splayed on the table between them as if ghosts were enjoying an evening game of Rummy. On the door before her hung a WELCOME sign haloed by an autumnal wreath, its faux berries like clusters of dark beady eyes. Under their scrutinizing gaze, she rang the doorbell.

She glanced over her shoulder, saw nothing out of the ordinary, and wondered what could have made her feel as though something lurked among the shadows. *Knowing the truth of things*, she supposed. Having come to know the reality of the world, the insidious truth that childhood innocence had kept hidden from her for seventeen years until it was swiftly revealed in the most agonizing of ways. Loved ones didn't live forever; best friends would sometimes become enemies; and worst of all, life had razor-sharp, poison-filled fangs that could pierce the human heart—*her* heart. And Katie knew, now, looking back the way she'd come, literally and figuratively, that darkness always reigned beyond the light.

It wasn't just *something* that was different, *everything* was different.

The door opened and the scent of spiced apples washed over her. Katie turned, closed her eyes and breathed it in. It reminded her of home, of sweet hugs and cookies in the oven. It reminded her of better times.

"Katie! Come in, come in." Mrs. Hapler opened the door wide. "Matthew will be right down."

Mrs. Hapler was made of sweetness and joy, the kind of woman you loved within minutes of meeting, as if you'd known her your whole life. Katie smiled, but before stepping inside, she held out her pillowcase...

"Trick or treat?"

Sighing, Mrs. Hapler said, "Matthew didn't tell you, did he? Never mind. I'm not surprised. Unfortunately, dear, we don't have any candy."

"Well, that's too bad." Katie stepped inside and Mrs. Hapler closed the door behind her. "Trick it is, then. May I borrow a roll of toilet paper?"

Mrs. Hapler laughed, warm and friendly. "Don't you even think about it!" She opened the refrigerator and removed a Diet Coke. "We don't usually get trick-or-treaters out here—you know how it is—so Harold and I have dinner reservations at Cassandra's, and then we're catching a late movie. If he ever gets out of the shower, that is. Would you like something to drink?"

"No, thank you."

"We bought candy our first year here, and no one came. Can you believe that?"

Katie nodded. Bridgetown Pines hadn't been conceived as a retirement community, but for all intents and purposes it had become one. The average age of its residents was just shy of dead. Few children ventured this far north of the city in hopes of getting a handful of wintergreen mints from a few old curmudgeons. And getting a handful of mints was a best-case scenario. The Haplers were the oddity of the neighborhood, still young and sprightly in their forties. Matt was the only kid on the block.

"Not a single person," Mrs. Hapler continued. She tapped the top of the soda can twice, opened it, and took a sip. "And with that big bowl of candy sitting on the table taunting us—I swear Harold and I gained ten pounds a day until it was all gone." She laughed. "But now with his diabetes and all... well, you understand."

Katie's face must have reflected the sadness she'd not yet found a way to hide when she was reminded of her father's passing, for Mrs. Hapler walked over, wrapped her in a loving embrace, and kissed the top of her head. "I'm sorry, dear. I wasn't thinking."

"It's okay," she said, fighting back tears that threatened to ruin her face paint. "I'm fine."

But she wasn't fine, and she wondered if she ever would be, if the sadness ever went away.

Her father had been a lifelong diabetic. Six months ago he'd gone to sleep, and he never woke. He just slipped away peacefully in the night. She could still remember the morning, the sun slicing through the gaps in her pink blinds, teasing her with its warmth as her mother's wails promised nothing but cold, cold, cold.

As devastated as Katie had been, the worst part of it all was that she'd lost not only her father, but her mother as well. At least it felt that way. Her mother shut down after her father's death, shut everyone and everything out of her life, and descended into a malignant darkness.

Just as the cold hands of despair were reaching up to pull her down into its black depths, Matt bounded into the room and brought a shining smile to her face—Mrs. Hapler's, too. He howled and snarled behind a rubber wolf-mask, making a real show of it. He wore a red-and-black plaid shirt, sleeves cut at the shoulders, and a black hooded sweatshirt underneath. His jeans were ragged and torn, as if he'd been attacked by one of his toothy brethren. A strip of synthetic wolf-hair, from forehead to shoulder, had been dyed green and hair-sprayed into a spiky spine.

"Nice hair," Katie said.

"It's a *wo*hawk," Matt replied, pausing for dramatic effect. "You see what I did there?

A punk-rock werewolf."

He howled again.

"Maybe you should join Team Jacob."

"Maybe I should eat your face," he said, pointing a wobbly elongated finger at her.

"Matthew," Mrs. Hapler said. "How many times have I told you, we don't eat our guests. Especially the nice ones."

"But that's what werewolves do!"

Mrs. Hapler looked at Katie, feigned a sad, contemplative face, and sighed heavily. "He has a point, you know, and since it is Halloween and all, I guess I'll make an exception. But—" she took another sip of her drink "—if you really must eat her face, please do it outside. I just mopped."

"Thanks, Mom! You're the best."

Katie laughed. They always knew how to make her laugh.

Katie and Matt gathered their things and said their good-byes.

"We'll be home sometime after midnight," said Mrs. Hapler. "You two behave, and be careful. And get me a Tootsie Roll."

Then they were out the door, racing

down the street and off into the night. They passed through the same field which Katie had come through earlier in the evening, intoxicated by the nostalgic promise of excitement and adventure.

They didn't see the pale-faced children creeping along the tree line.

* * *

Two hours later, with pillowcases full of sweet, sugary booty—Tootsie Pops, Smarties, Kit Kats, Snickers, Milky Ways, and so much more—Katie and Matt entered Bridgetown Pines and turned the corner at the far end of Farmington Circle.

Thick woods flanked both sides of the road, and a scant few streetlights did their futile best to hold back the shadows within. The branches overhead clacked like wind chimes constructed of bones. Around them, orange and yellow and red leaves lazily floated to their deaths, soft and peaceful.

"What the hell are we going to do with all this candy?" Katie shook her head, smiling.

"Well, I intend to eat it," Matt

said, removing his mask and gloves, the transformation back to human far less dramatic than depicted in movies. His face glistened with sweat. "I'm crazy like that."

Katie had a witty comeback lined up, but the words were swept away in a whirlwind of chatter that exploded within her head, suddenly, painfully, as if she had become hardwired into every cell network in the world—and everyone was shouting. Her eyes watered, knees buckled.

Matt dropped his pillowcase, reached out and steadied her. "Hey, you okay?"

Through the auditory haze, she saw Matt, his eyes wide with concern, and then looked past him, beyond the curve of the road. What she saw there both frightened and fascinated her, but reconciling those feelings amidst the bedlam in her head proved impossible. Waves of pain crashed against the inside of her skull, reverberating through her bones.

"Katie," Matt said. "What's wrong?"

The cacophonous buzzing and chatter in Katie's head dissipated, slowly, but words continued to fail her. Instead, she pointed.

Ahead, on Samantha Walker's front

lawn, stood a small cherubic figure, curiously strange, but equally horrifying. It was naked and without discernable genitalia, ghost-white skin shiny, smooth, like a small mannequin. Its arms were outstretched, hands cupped, cradling a long red candle, a teardrop of flame flickering above it. Wax glistened and dripped like blood between the child-thing's fingers, the contrast striking even in the dark.

The thing stared at them, eyes unblinking, black and emotionless, almost alien.

Something screamed through the quiet but still present static in Katie's head—*run run RUN!* it seemed to say—but her legs refused to budge.

When Matt turned and saw the thing staring at them, he flinched, leaned back as if preparing to bolt. "What the crap is that?"

Katie cleared her throat, found her voice again. "I don't know. What do *you* think it is?"

"No idea." Matt craned his neck forward and scrunched up his face. "Was it there before?"

"I don't think so," Katie said. She glanced

down the street, and gasped. "Oh my God, Matt, look! They're everywhere."

There were nine houses on Farmington Circle, all clustered near its circular end. Katie had always felt close to her father here. He'd helped build every house on the street, and they stood a testament to the man he had been—quiet, strong, sheltering. She felt protected in their presence.

Now, standing before each of those homes was a perfectly still child clutching a dark red candle, and Katie no longer felt safe.

"I don't get it." Matt shook his head.

She didn't get it, either, but she felt a jagged blade of fear scraping its way down her spine. She loved horror—books, movies, music—but the image before her was too spooky, too real.

A darkness comes, child, a single voice said, entering her mind uninvited, as smooth and cold as an icicle.

"What?" she said.

"I said—"

"No. Not you."

Matt cocked an eyebrow, made a fist, and spoke into it: "Crazy Katie Bananas, this is Big Daddy Matt, come again? Over. *Ksssh*."

The blade grew still at the small of her back, its tip piercing her skin with slow, steady persistence.

"Did you hear anything?" she asked, unable to look away from the child.

Matt's brow crinkled like a pile of discarded wrapping paper on Christmas morning. "You okay?"

"Never mind," she said, massaging her temples. "I don't like this."

"Word up on that, sista. This is either a stupid joke, or everyone on this street is in a weirdo cult. Maybe both. Sure you're okay?"

She nodded. But Katie couldn't shake the feeling that something beyond their understanding, something unnatural—even supernatural—was happening. A big pill to swallow, but the alternative—that she was bat-shit crazy—was much bigger, and she wasn't quite ready to gulp that one down.

"Can we go?"

"Yeah, sure."

Matt picked up his candy, and together they walked into the unknown.

• • •

Matt crossed the front lawn of his home, his movements bold and purposeful. His footsteps darkened the dew-covered grass with each step. As he drew closer to the figure, he slowed, hesitated, and then stopped a few feet away.

You must run, flee. A darkness comes.

"Matthew," Katie said, tugging on his arm like a toddler trying to get her mother's attention. "Can we *please* go inside?"

She looked back over her shoulder, half-expecting to see an army of porcelain-skinned children creeping up on them, claws and fangs bared. But still they stood, one on each front lawn, blank-faced and unmoving.

"It's fake," Matt declared. He was staring into the black orbs that served as the child's eyes. "Christ, what a bizarre prank." He chuckled, though Katie could tell it was a nervous kind of laughter.

"Matthew, I think it's real." She wasn't sure why she believed this, because it made no more sense than any other tale this holiday had been built upon, but she knew it was true. She *felt* it, somehow, heard it loud and clear.

"What? Come on! It's fake," he insisted. "Probably a plastic Halloween prop—a weird one—or some wacky Japanese candleholder. They never get that shit right."

"I'm hearing a voice, something...I don't know, Matt, but I don't like it. We have to go."

"Go where? I thought—"

"Inside!"

Behind Matt and his incredulous stare, the child's mouth opened impossibly wide. A panicked squeal escaped Katie's lips. She lurched backward, stumbled over one of Mrs. Hapler's juniper shrubs that adorned the lawn, and landed hard on her backside.

Matt spun around, screamed when he saw the gaping mouth, and defensively swung his candy-laden pillowcase. It slammed into the child's chest, and the candle tumbled from its grasp, flame flickering to nothing as it rolled across the wet lawn.

As if in response, the voice in Katie's head sliced through her like a hail of razors, no words, just an agonizing howl—and she howled with it.

The child's eyes cataracted before

them. Its statuesque stance faltered, and it crumpled to the ground. A few inches away, a curl of smoke rose from the crimson candle, disappeared into the night like a spirit called home.

Katie scrambled to her feet, her pillowcase and candy forgotten among the shrubbery.

"Did you see that?" Matt said, nearly screeching the words. "Jumpin' Jesus on a pogo stick! Did you *see* that?"

"I saw," she said, wishing it were a lie.

Matt turned around, and Kate watched the color drain from his face like a cartoon character seeing a ghost, as if he were becoming one of the mysterious children.

"Holy goddamn crap," he whispered.

"I'm okay," she said.

"Not you. Look."

Katie followed his gaze and the blade of fear sliced through her spine, paralyzing her.

A soft orange glow spread across James Rothney's front lawn. There, another child stood, surrounded by the delicate light of a fire—which emanated not from without but from *within* its body! Its eyes were deep pools of flickering fire, its skin the pink-orange of a midsummer sunset. The child stood at attention, hands dripping with what appeared to be blood. The candle was gone.

Up and down the street, the children stood still as soldiers, sentries burning with an inner fire, like pumpkins.

Like pumpkins...

Pumpkins...

It echoed through the halls of her mind... and then she understood.

Katie had attributed her fear to the mere presence of the children, but all at once the shades of ignorance lifted and the sunshiny rays of realization illuminated her thoughts: The children weren't there to harm them.

Like fucking pumpkins!

"My god," she said. "What have you done?"

Katie rushed past Matt, and fell to her knees beside the seemingly lifeless ghostchild. "Help me," she said. "Quickly!"

The child's hands were streaked with red, as though it had been freshly crucified, its body tossed aside for scavengers to feast upon. Katie's hand closed around the child's fingers, now paler than before, and a cold river flooded her veins, stomped through her bones like Death marching. She gasped for air.

And then the voice came again, unbidden as before, with such urgency it threatened to unhinge her sanity.

Darkness! You must flee the darkness, child! They come!

The world around her flickered like an old television transmission. She clenched her eyes tight, and her mind filled with the image of her father, smiling, radiant. He held his finger to his lips, like he had done so many times before when he wanted her to stop talking and just listen. The scene within her mind faded to Bridgetown Pines, as if she were standing in the middle of Farmington Circle with a million compound eyes at her disposal, each one helping piece together fragments of one scene...

The ghostly procession emerges from the woods, and one by one the strange beings split from the group to stand like watchmen around the homes of the Pines' residents...

Some turn and face the street, while others

disappear behind the homes...

They hold out their palms like children collecting snowflakes...

Drops of red fall from the sky, into their upturned hands, and the red rises, rises, rises, until finally a single flaming teardrop descends from the heavens, burning bright...

Katie and Matt appear at the far end of the street, they linger in front of Samantha's house, and then they're standing before the child on Matt's front lawn...

And then...

And then...

And then the darkness moves...

Thick strips of black break away from the shadows, undulating through the air like heartworms heading for the heart of the world. Bloodcurdling whispers echo down the street as if all the damned souls of Hell were marching to war, singing songs of deliverance...

The mass of shadows turn as one...

Katie's eyes jerked open. For a moment she thought she was emerging from a nightmare, safe and sound under a tangle of blankets and the warm sun peeking through the blinds of her bedroom window.

But there was no sun, no warmth, just an icy realization that, if anything, the nightmare had just begun.

* * *

"What the hell, Katie?" Matt knelt beside her, a look of profound fear and confusion contorting his face—an emotional reflection of that which tore at her insides.

The sweet smells of myriad candies floated up Katie's nostrils and down her throat, and she had to swallow to keep from throwing up. "What happened?"

"You tell me," he said. "First you're scolding me like I'm two, and then you're grabbing onto this stupid thing, twitching and muttering like a lunatic. What the hell?"

"How long was I like that?"

"I don't know. Ten, maybe twenty seconds."

Katie tried to resolve that in her muddled head. How had she seen so much in such a short period of time? She looked down at the child and the vision returned, this time from her own memory. She saw the black things detach from the shadows, twisting through the trees. She saw her father...

Could it really have been him?

Her mind reeled.

She looked toward Samantha's place. Samantha, who had recently lost her daughter—her only child—at the hands of an unlicensed drunk driver. And James Rothney's father had just passed, at the age of 101, outliving all his siblings by two decades. Katie's mind moved from house to house. Carmen Langford...husband...lung cancer. Dead. Garret Wilson...son...overdose. Dead. Melinda and Ray Kingsbury, Ian Millhouse, Sarah Forest...each of them had recently lost family members.

"Unlock the door," she said. "We need to get inside."

"Are you listening to yourself? Jesus Christ! You're going crazy right before my frickin' eyes."

"Now!"

Spurred on by her commanding tone, Matt thrust his hand in his pocket, pulled out his keys, and stepped past her, his face twisted into an aggravated sneer. He made to kick the prone child on the lawn, but seemed to think better of it, and headed toward the house.

Katie turned and watched the child holding vigil on Samantha's lawn down the street. The fire burned strong from within, but then, ever so slightly, it dimmed as if battling a biting wind. The flame shivered and pulsed and faltered to an ember.

Then, slowly, like the awakening of dawn, the small glow within the child brightened, brightened, and brightened more, until it repelled the darkness once again.

As if warding off evil spirits...

As if the vision she saw through the eyes of the fallen child had come true.

Though she couldn't see anything now, she knew that the flickering of light was a battle being waged and that the darkness had been repulsed by whatever force the child commanded.

Darkness comes, she thought.

It was only a matter of time before that darkness got to Matt's house.

Katie crossed the lawn and took all three porch steps in one stride. Inside, Matt pulled out a chair at the kitchen table. He sat down heavily, grabbed a Red Delicious from the centerpiece, and began rolling it back and forth between his hands.

"I need fire," Katie said.

"You need therapy," Matt said, not looking up.

"Shut up and help me, Matthew! We haven't got time."

"Time for *what*, exactly?" He stared at her, defiant. The apple rolled to a stop before him like a heart that had ceased beating. "Are you in on this prank—trying to creep me out, scare me?"

"It's not a goddamn prank," she said, crossing the kitchen to stand before him. She softened her voice, hoping to calm his nerves. "The thing on the lawn, the child, it's here to protect us—they're here to protect everyone."

"Oh, right. Of course!" He slapped the tabletop. "It all makes sense now."

Katie ignored him. She told him of her vision, the black things, her father, everything, and when she finished she had to admit, it sounded downright nutso.

"And you think it's real," he said.

She nodded, ignoring his derisive tone. Crazy-sounding or not, Katie didn't *think* anything. She *knew*. Her father had come to her from a place beyond this world, free of disease, free of pain, happy. The children were some sort of avatars, manifest protectors, sent by her father and by the recently-passed family members of Matt's neighbors. She knew it with all her heart.

As if reading her thoughts, intent on shattering them, Matt asked: "But what about the Samson's? They're *both* dead now."

Katie's confidence deflated, she felt stupid, like a little girl naively believing in fairy tales. Matt was right. Mr. Samson had died two days ago after a short bout with pneumonia; his funeral was being held Tuesday afternoon. Her theory had a gaping hole from which reason bled freely. Matt hadn't lost any family members, either.

Despite her desire to believe, skepticism of an afterlife—Heaven and Hell, and all that religious hoo-ha—slammed against her newfound hope.

But she was here, and her father *had*

passed. There was that. She wanted to—had to—believe it was possible, that her sweet, gentle father was somehow still looking out for her.

Her mind raced, and her thoughts ricocheted through her head in a tangled mess of self-doubt.

Matt's smug smile hurt.

"Molly," she said, grasping for an answer. But it made sense. Sort of.

"Really. A dog?"

"Yeah, a dog. A dog that's *alive*!" Molly was still alive, still living in the Samson's home. Paula Bell, their neighbor, had been feeding and walking her since Mr. Samson was admitted to the hospital. It was a stretch, but could the Samson's be protecting their dog? Of course they could. Molly had been like a child to them.

Or maybe it wasn't so simple. *Goddamn!* If only she could put the pieces together...

"You're nuts." Matt laughed, a good old *guffaw*. "Crazy-looking midget angels descend from Heaven to protect...wait for it—" he held up a finger "—a dog."

And us, she wanted to shout. She had the

urge to smack him, right across his smirking face. She loved his sense of humor, his ability to turn even the most mundane things into an adventure, but sometimes he just didn't listen. Usually it was over something so trivial it didn't matter.

But *this* mattered. *Now* mattered.

So she reached across the table and smacked him, the sharp *crack* echoing throughout the kitchen. Matt's head jerked to the side and a splotch of red spread across his cheek like a five-fingered disease. He turned back toward her, jaw muscles twitching, the shock of it all blurring behind the tears twinkling in his eyes. He blinked to keep the tears from falling.

"I'm sorry," she said. "I'm so sorry. But you have to listen to me."

"You hit me," he said in barely a whisper.

"I'm *really* sorry." She reached out and squeezed his hand. "But you really need to listen. You saw that thing move. You saw it with your own eyes. I'm *not* crazy. I'm not! We're in danger, Matthew. From what, I don't know, but it's not good. Trust me, please."

He remained quiet for a long time, and

it took all that Katie had not to prod him along. "Fine," he said, his voice like a soft breeze.

"Thank you." She pulled him to his feet. "We need a lighter, and quickly."

Moving zombielike, he said, "One fire utensil coming right up," and pulled a purple barbecue lighter from the kitchen drawer. He followed Katie outside.

A few feet away from where the child lay in the cold, wet grass, she found the candle. It smelled of old copper. A tender kind of warmth flowed into her when she picked it up, and she smiled.

"Lift it," she said, pointing to the body at Matt's feet.

He hesitated. "For what?"

"Stop asking questions, will you? Just do it." She was running on adrenaline and instinct.

Grabbing hold of the child, Matt inhaled sharply and groaned as if he'd been punched in the stomach. His body stiffened, twitched. The green of his eyes disappeared, his pupils stretching into sightless black orbs. Drool slithered from the corner of his mouth like a glass snake and shattered on the grass below. He lurched upright, gasping for air, flailing his arms to find his balance.

"Christ," he said. "Holy fuckersucks!"

"What happened?" Katie said.

"Wow."

Matt stared down the street, wide-eyed. Katie thought about slapping him a second time. "Matt, *focus!* What happened? What did you see?"

"Too much," he said, turning toward her, his lips trembling. His eyes were wide with fear, but finally focused. "They've seen us."

"Oh no." Hands shaking, Katie flicked the lighter. The flame sputtered. She kept at it, and it caught on the third try. She held it to the candle.

There was no wick.

No, she thought.

She placed the flame directly to the candle's tip. Nothing happened. It wouldn't catch.

No, no, no!

"Here," Matt said. "Try this."

Kneeling, he hoisted the child to a

sitting position. The child's body hung limply, its head bowed. Grabbing its hands, Matt placed them together, palms up, as if accepting sacramental bread.

Katie stood there, staring into the sky, waiting for the blood-red raindrops to fall, like they had in her vision. But again, nothing happened.

Her heart plummeted.

"Give it the candle," Matt said. "Hurry."

She silently cursed herself. This wasn't your everyday candle. She should have known better. Instantly the child reacted when she placed the candle in its palms. Its body stiffened as if air were being blown into a balloon. With Matt's help, it stood. Eyes shifted from white to black.

Matt let go and stepped back.

Flee...now...

The voice was weaker, but the urgency still clear.

Matt grabbed Kate's arm. "Let's go!"

They ran the short distance to the house. Once inside, Matt slammed the door shut, locked it, and turned out the lights. Through the window they watched a single drop of fire descend from the sky like a dying firefly.

As if in prayer, the ghostly sentinel bowed its head.

The air around them seemed to gasp, and a fiery glow pulsed within the child. It grew brighter, stronger, hungrier, the air shimmering and blurring like waves of heat over a desert highway, until all was bathed in a dazzling orange hue.

Matt went to the kitchen sink and splashed water on his face. "Holy crap," he said. "Katie, come check this out."

He had moved the curtain aside and was looking out the window that faced the back yard. There, too, stood one of the strange children, surrounded by the beautiful orange sheen. Two more stood silently on either side of the house, making four in total, all afire from within, a protective dome encapsulating the house.

They moved to the front window again and watched the street beyond. Though they couldn't see the wormlike shadows, nor could they truly fathom the danger, they knew where they were by the way the firelight dimmed as the dark things repeatedly tried to break through the near invisible walls that kept them at bay.

Matt pulled Katie close, and kissed her forehead. "I'm sorry," he said.

She embraced him, not sure what to say. The kiss, innocent as it might have been, had sent her heart aflutter. "It's okay," she said quietly.

"So now what do we do?"

"I don't know." Katie hadn't had time to process what had already happened, let alone figure out what they should do next. Halloween had come alive in ways more real than she could ever have imagined, shattering the fictional barrier that usually separated her world from that of the dark. "We wait, I guess."

She rested her head on Matt's shoulder.

He hugged her a little tighter.

The minutes ticked by and they watched their little corner of the world through the unbelievable orange sphere.

Again Katie thought of her father. She'd felt lost since his death, but had tried to remain strong. Her mother had dealt with the loss in a completely different way—isolation, denial, anger—and Katie's relationship with her had suffered greatly.

But maybe her father was still here with them. Perhaps, with Katie's help, her mother would soon emerge from the darkness into which she had descended.

Perhaps.

Katie had always wanted to trust in what the religious folk preached, but it had always seemed so hokey. Now, however, it seemed wonderful. The possibilities warmed her heart. And even if it weren't entirely true, or not true at all, could believing in some higher power, having faith in it, be so terrible?

One thing she did know—beyond the window, past the strange child and the enchanting sphere, there lurked a darkness more menacing than she could ever have imagined before tonight.

She closed her eyes, thought of her father, found hope for her mother, and dared to believe.

K. Allen Wood's fiction has appeared in *52 Stitches, Vol. 2, The Zombie Feed, Epitaphs: The Journal of New England Horror Writers, The Gate 2: 13 Tales of Isolation and Despair, Anthology Year One, Appalachian Undead* and its companion chapbook, *Mountain Dead,* and most recently in *Anthology Year Two: Inner Demons Out.* He lives and plots in Massachusetts.

For more info, visit www.kallenwood.com.

HOWLING THROUGH THE KEYHOLE

The stories behind the stories.

"Halloween On..."

Halloween is my favorite holiday for a lot of reasons, but chief among them is that it is a night for people to empower themselves by assuming an identity *they* choose. Sure, it's an occasion for children to go door to door begging for treats and for college students to dress up as sexy Freddy Kruegers and bad puns like "cereal killers" before getting wasted. But for a lot of us, it is a day to be something we always wanted to be, if only for a few hours. Unlike all other holidays, it's a day about individual self-determination and wish fulfillment.

The inspiration for both of my pieces in "Halloween On..." comes from the idea that Halloween is a chance to try on a new skin and reinvent yourself. Both of my characters, Nick and Bonnie, are defined and confined by the contrast between who they are and who they want to be. On the corner of Cave and Ellis, and at the other end of the neighborhood on Ballard Ave., I tried to offer twin stories of the struggle to assert one's own identity. Nick is a bullied, scared child, who lives in self-imposed isolation. At first it might appear that he's preparing for something awful by playing his game, but in reality he's confronting his fears—forging himself into the man he wants to be. Bonnie, by contrast, lives in isolation as a result of her husband's obsession with their showpiece home. She wants to engage with the outside world and invite it in, but he won't let her. When she confines him instead, she throws the door to her own cage wide open.

Whether or not you sympathize with either of these characters, my intent was to offer a glimpse at people who wear masks every day, except on Halloween, when they are able to be who they really are.

—*Bracken MacLeod*

I like Halloween. I like candy. With "The

186

Corner of Ash and Thomas Streets," I wanted to do a nod to the most cliché of Halloween creepies, the candy tamperer. And I named the streets for one of my favorite current writers, Lee Thomas. On "The Corner of Kenwood Lane," named for my brother from another mother, Ken Wood, I went for the sad. I sometimes do that. And...I like candy.

–John Boden

"Night in the Forest of Loneliness"

"She told him her name was Willow, and he laughed and claimed his name was Oak."

I wrote that line on a printed copy of another short story and some months later it led to "Night in the Forest of Loneliness," my first flash piece.

–David G. Blake

"Out of Field Theory"

The idea for "Out of Field Theory" came when a graduate class I was taking—Film &

Philosophy—was studying the philosophy of Gilles Deleuze. I probably understood it just as well as my protagonist did—not very well at all—but one of his ideas about framing struck a chord in me. Framing suggests that, when we take or film an image or movie, we're creating an alternate reality that's not necessarily bound by the frames we artificially impose on it. The idea that we were creating a reality, and that it continued past the frame of a picture or movie, proved very unsettling, and after a year or two of germination, produced "Out of Field Theory."

–*Kevin Lucia*

"Tricks and Treats"

Thinking about Halloween, I always remember being a kid and going trick-or-treating. Dressing up in a costume, pretending that you're someone or some*thing* else, and getting to go door to door where people you don't even know give you handfuls of sweets. What could be better?

I also remember when I was informed I

was too old to go trick-or-treating anymore. No more free goodies, no more running around in the dark trying to scare my friends or the neighbors. Yet not quite old enough to be into parties or doing what the older kids did on that magical night.

That was the background of the story, just that reminiscence of more innocent times. But there are always those who aren't ready to give up the free stuff, and who are willing to ruin another child's fond memories of that favorite holiday. And then I got to thinking... what if there are other things out there, whose ideas of trick-or-treating are altogether darker and less innocuous? It's always good to remember, we're not the only ones out there wandering in the shadows.

—Rose Blackthorn

"Howdy Doody Time"

We moved into a new house recently, and, as an adult, I've never lived in a place that had proper trick-or-treating, so I was having some anxiety as to how to prepare—are there a lot of kids? How much candy should I get? What kind? Are they going to egg us if we don't have Snickers? Those kinds of things. That's about it.

–Kriscinda Lee Everitt

"Before This Night Is Done"

My parents got me Danny Elfman's film score for *Batman Returns* (1992) at some point in the mid-to-late 90s, but it wasn't until after I got my first portable CD player in the later 90s, that I really listened to it. I began to discover multiple musical surprises on it; besides the obvious sweeping, heroic themes and a number of more bombastic sections for the more action-oriented scenes in the movie. I was mystified by the dark passages in tracks like "The Lair, Pt. 1" and "Selena Transforms." In fact, I became downright *fascinated* by these tracks; they crawled with nocturnal soundscapes, and with repeated listens (independent of the movie), I swear, the tracks got even *darker*. I became determined to somehow interpret and share the dark imagery inspired by Mr. Elfman's score, and with "Before This Night Is Done," that darkness has crawled out of my ears and onto the page.

–*Barry Lee Dejasu*

"Allhallowtide (To the Faithless Departed)"

I keep a folder by my desk with old poetry, artwork, and other ramblings from my youth—a keyhole of my own, if you will, one that looks into my past. Now and then I'll go through and find a piece I feel might have some substance to it, and that's what happened here. I played with the stream of consciousness narrative and reworked it into a more experimental form to try to give the speaker a more distinct voice while still conveying the chaotic nature of the piece. It was originally called "Fear", and struck me as fitting for a Halloween issue once I explored the theme of religion a bit further and fleshed out the connections. (Well, in my own mind, anyway...) And to be perfectly honest, it's pretty surreal seeing a poem go

to print twenty-five years after writing it—
perhaps more so than the poem itself.

—Sydney Leigh

"The Candle Eaters"

Stephen King once said, "If it's a bad idea,
you'll forget about it; if it's a good idea, it will
stick around." I tend to agree.

Before writing "The Candle Eaters," the
basic premise had been germinating in my
head for years. Every Halloween I'd think, I
really need to write this story someday, and
then inevitably the day would pass and I'd
vow to do it next year. Rinse. Repeat.

Finally, back in 2010, a small-press
magazine (of which I am a big fan) announced
that they were putting out a Halloween issue,
and I wanted to be a part of it.

The first version of "The Candle Eaters"
missed the mark. With thinly-drawn
characters, a darker feel overall, and an
ending full of death and destruction, it was
not the "good idea" that had been in my head
for all those years. With no time for a rewrite,

however, I made the amateurish mistake and submitted it anyway—and was promptly rejected (by one of this issue's contributors, in fact).

What I did accomplish with that first version, I think, was introduce some original elements to the oft-explored Halloween setting. Specifically the "candle eaters," which of course are a riff on the old-time tradition of using hollowed-out turnips or pumpkins to ward off evil spirits.

On the surface, the story included here isn't drastically different from that first version, but I think it accomplishes what I had initially envisioned so long ago, which was a story fundamentally about faith and hope without being overly sentimental.

Ultimately, I just hope "The Candle Eaters" is a good, entertaining story.

–K. Allen Wood

Additional Bios

John Langan is the author of two collections, *The Wide, Carnivorous Sky and Other Monstrous Geographies* (**Hippocampus** 2013) and *Mr. Gaunt and Other Uneasy Encounters* (**Prime** 2008). He has written a novel, *House of Windows* (**Night Shade** 2009), and, with Paul Tremblay, has co-edited an anthology, *Creatures: Thirty Years of Monsters* (**Prime** 2011). He lives in upstate New York with his wife, younger son, and a menagerie.

·

Babs Boden is the youngest and accidental daughter of Fritz and Syl. Born and raised in the wilds of the Pennsylvania chocolate regions, she spent her formative years being surly, smirking, making wildly sarcastic comments at breathtakingly inappropriate moments, and fending off crazed Pentecostals armed only with a Joan Jett 45 and a bottle of Aussie Sprunch.

She earns her living sitting in a little gray cube at a soulless corporation running SAS, configuring databases, and making snide remarks. She is currently on husband #1, has two male children whom she has so far managed not to sell to the circus, and no pets.

One day she hopes to retire, obtain her CDL, and become a long-haul trucker.

•

Jeremy Wagner writes lyrics and music and tours worldwide with the death metal band **Broken Hope**. He also writes horror fiction. He has been published in *RIP Magazine*, *Terrorizer*, *Metal Edge*, *Microhorror*, and has had work published through **Perseus Books**, **St. Martin's Press**, and **Ravenous Romance Publishers**.

Wagner's most recent published works include his debut novel, *The Armageddon Chord*; the short story "Romance Ain't Dead," which appears in the zombie-romance anthology

Hungry for Your Love; and the short story "The Creatures from Craigslist" in the anthology *Fangbangers: An Erotic Anthology of Fangs, Claws, Sex and Love*.

He currently has two new novels under revision.

∗

Lee Thomas is the Lambda Literary Award- and Bram Stoker Award-winning author of *The Dust of Wonderland*, *In the Closet Under the Bed*, *The German*, *Torn*, *Ash Street*, *Like Light for Flies*, and *Butcher's Road*. Lee lives in Austin, Texas.

You can find him online at www. leethomasauthor.com.

∗

Mike Lombardo is an indie filmmaker/FX artist who runs **Reel Splatter Productions**. His short films have been played at film festivals across the US and overseas. His newest film, *The Stall,* a Lovecraftian tale of a man trapped in a public restroom during the apocalypse, just finished its festival tour and is available at www.reelsplatter.com. You should buy a copy. Seriously, that would be totally boss.

SILENT Q DESIGN

Silent Q Design was founded in Montreal in 2006 by **Mikio Murakami.** Melding together the use of both realistic templates and surreal imagery, Mikio's artistry proves, at first glance, that a passion for art still is alive, and that no musician, magazine, or venue should suffer from the same bland designs that have been re-hashed over and over.

Mikio's work has been commissioned both locally and internationally, by bands such as **Redemption, Synastry, Starkweather,** and **Epocholypse.** *Shock Totem #3* was his first book design project.

For more, visit **www.silentqdesign.net.**

ALSO AVAILABLE FROM SHOCK TOTEM PUBLICATIONS

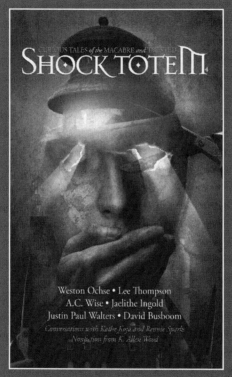

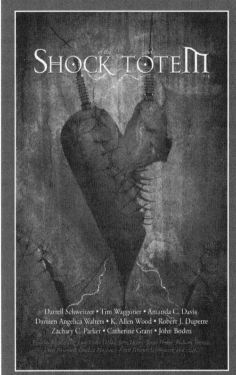

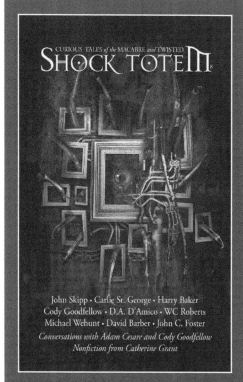

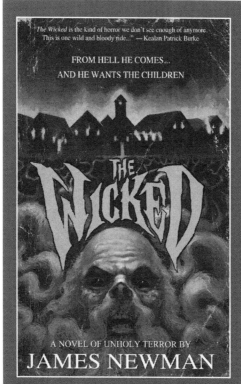

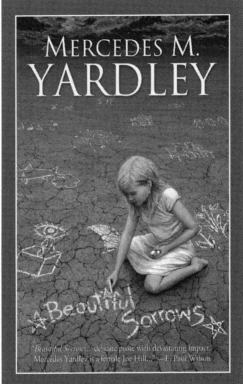

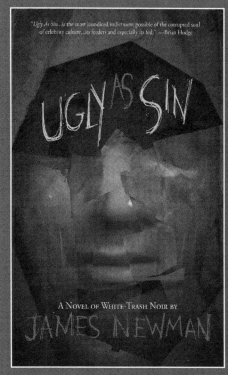

ALSO AVAILABLE FROM SHOCK TOTEM PUBLICATIONS

DOMINOES
JOHN BODEN

AVAILABLE EXCLUSIVELY IN PRINT FORMAT
www.SHOCKTOTEM.com

FIND US ONLINE

http://www.shocktotem.com

http://www.twitter.com/shocktotem

http://www.facebook.com/shocktotem

http://www.youtube.com/
shocktotemmag

Made in the USA
San Bernardino, CA
29 September 2016